LAIRD OF MISRULE

The Enchanted Well Series
Book 1

Mary Wine

ARE YOU SIGNED UP FOR DRAGONBLADE'S BLOG?

You'll get the latest news and information on exclusive giveaways, exclusive excerpts, coming releases, sales, free books, cover reveals and more.

Check out our complete list of authors, too!

No spam, no junk. That's a promise!

Sign Up Here

www.dragonbladepublishing.com

Dearest Reader;

Thank you for your support of a small press. At Dragonblade Publishing, we strive to bring you the highest quality Historical Romance from some of the best authors in the business. Without your support, there is no 'us', so we sincerely hope you adore these stories and find some new favorite authors along the way.

Happy Reading!

CEO, Dragonblade Publishing

Additional Dragonblade books by Author Mary Wine

The Enchanted Well Series
Laird of Misrule (Book 1)
Once Upon an Enchanted Well (Novella)

Highland Rogues Series
The Highlander's Demand (Book 1)
The Highlander's Destiny (Book 2)
The Highlander's Captive (Book 3)
The Highlander's Promise (Book 4)

Also from Mary Wine
Midnight Flame (Novella)

Foreword

The Eight Years War, or the War of Rough Wooing, was started by Henry VIII, who wanted to stop an alliance between France and Scotland. This union would have afforded the French access to Scotland, from where they could launch an invasion into England. The Scottish king died early in this conflict, passing the crown to his newborn daughter Mary Stuart.

Scotland was split between a French marriage alliance and an English one. The core of this disagreement was the matter of religion—the Church of Rome or Protestantism. Between 1544 and 1550, much of lowland Scotland was occupied by English troops intent on finding the baby queen, to take her to England, so she would be raised as a Protestant.

Edinburgh was burned, and numerous other towns suffered the same fate. Scots were forced to become "Assured Men", bound by contract to defend the English marriage. Mary Stuart was smuggled out of Scotland at five years of age, and sent to France, where she was raised in the Catholic faith.

Peace was restored in 1550, but much blood had been spilt. The topic of religion divided the lowland Scots, and trust would take a long time to be restored.

When Henry VIII's son, Edward, died without issue, his sister Mary Tudor took the throne of England in 1553. She belonged to the Church of Rome and began to enforce a return to this faith. England had been a haven for those who embraced the break with the Catholic Church under Henry VIII, but suddenly, they had to recant or flee.

The lowlands of Scotland were also torn in this battle between faiths. The only stability laid in clan allegiance. Castles offered protection from invading troops, while clansmen manned the walls, and rode the land to protect their clan members.

It was a time when anything could happen. And sometimes, it did.

CHAPTER ONE

Borderland, 1554

Prudence and her family were in hiding.

Wales might officially be within the borders of England, but it was a wild land, one that had never really been bent to obedience by those sitting on the throne in London.

Seven long years of war had left its mark on the land, and its inhabitants did not trust one another. They kept to their farms, filling their days with labor, and savoring the peace. Even if they all knew that the land they worked on was disputed. The only certainty in their lives was the fact that at some point, war would return.

It all seemed so very far away, but Prudence knew she'd be wise to remember the threat was very, very real.

Trust no one. Don't draw attention to yourself. Live quietly...silently really. Those were the words she lived by now. Well, she and her entire family.

The wind blew hard and cold, cutting right through the layers of her clothing. Winter was approaching, and soon, whatever food that remained unharvested would be lost—something they could ill afford if they wanted to survive through the long winter months.

Prudence rolled her shoulders to ease the ache between her shoulder blades and reached for another bundle of stocks. The barley had been beaten from them and stored and now, she was set the task of removing the chaff to make the fibers ready to be wound into rope.

It was hard work—toil that made her ache from head to toe.

Because she and her family had recently arrived from outside of London, she'd never done work like this before, but it was hardly difficult to understand. She grabbed the stalks and slapped them into a troth that was standing up as high as her head. There was a center beam which was attached to the troth with a rod so it might open and close. She slammed it down on the reeds, pulling and pushing the bundle about until all of the outer husk was broken away from the inner fibers. The first few were always fun, a bit like she was freeing the fibers from captivity.

But only the first few.

By the time she reached for the last bundle, the soft spots on her hands had become blisters. Hopefully, next season, they might turn to calluses. It would be less painful at least.

Each day was the same. Not a bit of sunlight might be wasted for rope could be sold.

Her younger brothers would arrive from time to time, to collect all of her bundles, and take them down to where her other sisters were combing the fibers straight. Then the bundles would be spun into thin rope, which would be combined into thicker rope.

It was the last of the harvest work.

Back in London, harvest used to be a fun time. All of nature's bounty made for full supper tables and homes filled with rich aromas. The harbor would be full of ships arriving from their voyages, filled with spices, sugar, citrus fruit, and too many delicacies to name!

Aye, back before your name was Prudence...

Though she didn't care for her Puritan name, she was happy that her father seemed to believe following the staunch Puritan religion ensured their household heavenly grace. Or perhaps it was more direct to just say that her father believed that he now had sons, because he'd pleased God with his new choice of worship.

That does not make up for being called Prudence...or the fact that your father wanted a son more than you.

No, it did not. She'd much preferred Braylin. And what was so wrong with having daughters over sons? So long as the child was healthy and the mother strong? Life was such a beautiful thing. It seemed to her that getting caught up in the details of gender was such a waste.

She knew her father would not agree with her.

Still, her family had more important things to dwell upon now—such as avoiding being arrested. Back in London, the new queen was set upon bringing back the Catholic faith. In fact, Mary Tudor considered it her duty to enforce compliance to the church. Hence, Prudence and her family had fled to Wales, and prayed daily for obscurity.

The wind blew again, almost as though it was telling Prudence that she was indeed seen. A little tingle went down her spine, leaving behind a sense of foreboding. There was naught but trees and harvested fields in sight, yet Prudence didn't feel forgotten or hidden.

Oh, there was also a well.

The well was still in good repair. It was constructed of stone, which was covered over by green moss, and stood near a patch of huge, ancient oak trees. Whoever had built it was long gone. It was strange that there was no dwelling near it at all.

It stood silently alone, like something from a minstrel's song.

"Come back at moonrise if you want to know the real worth of that well."

Prudence jumped. Norla, the older woman who kept the house they now lived in, was standing near her.

Norla winked and smiled broadly. Her face was wrinkled by time, but her eyes sparkled with the memory of youth. She pointed at the well.

"That is the midnight well—it is enchanted. If ye eat a piece of forest fruit and look into a bucket of water with the full moon overhead, ye shall see the face of yer true love."

Prudence looked back at the well. She really should not have, and yet, somehow, the possibilities it held were irresistible.

Was that the source of her feelings of being watched? Prudence took a step toward it without realizing that she'd moved.

Norla laughed. "Not tonight girl. The moon won't be full for another two days. Do not ever drink from that well unless it's beneath a full moon, for just as it bestows gifts of sight, the rest of the time, the water from its depths will chill yer bones, and freeze yer heart, allowing no room for love."

Norla left a small pottery jug near Prudence's feet.

"Mind my words…" Norla's tone changed to one of warning. "Ye are new to this land, which has never been fully tamed. English, Welsh, Norseman, Saxon, and Scot mingle here. We do as we want, since the royals are too far away to control us."

Norla held up two of her fingers. "I'll leave the fruit on the well for ye. Don't stop once ye start, but eat it all, and then close yer eyes, and look into the water in the bucket. Mind me girl… Empty yer mind. Do not try to guide the well, lest you be drawn onto the path to bitterness."

PRUDENCE DID HER best not to think about Norla's words. And she certainly wouldn't go up to the well seeking guidance.

It was folly to believe in enchantments.

Still, it had been so long since she'd been afforded any merriment, and the thought that the well might bring happiness to her was hard to put aside. It had been ten years since her father had despaired of having any sons and taken to finding a means of pleasing the Lord. The transformation of their way of life hadn't been instantaneous. It had happened over several years.

And now that her three brothers were here, the somber demeanor of the family was complete, for her parents believed the

Lord had made good on his end of the bargain. So, the family would keep the staunch rules of the Puritan faith, as promised.

You love your brothers…

She did.

But she was getting close to the age for marriage, and she had a growing fear that her father would wed her to one of his Puritan friends.

Of course, he's going to keep you in the faith…

Her inner voice was likely correct…which left Prudence looking at a bleak future. She'd be forever more known as Prudence and expected to be meek and obedient. It wasn't that she was wild, but a bit of fun now and again was definitely something she longed for.

You could go to the well…

To see what? The face of a somber Puritan groom?

Or perhaps the fairies who enchant the well will work their magic on you….

Her mother and father would be horrified by the notion. They'd think she was going mad to even consider trying such a thing.

The full moon only comes up at night…

True. Her parents had taken to locking the shutters and doors against the evil spirits that came with the darkness. There was no reason, short of a fire, to ever open a door after the sun set. And that rule was even stricter now that they were on the border-lands, where it was rumored witchery was still practiced. And even more feared than sorcery were the Scots who roamed the land.

Well, Norla did tell you she'd leave some fruit for you…

Prudence thought about Norla. She knew the older woman wouldn't suggest she go to the Midnight Well if there as any chance of danger. Did she dare? Inside her chest, Prudence felt her heart beating harder, faster than it had in months. Her blood was speeding through her veins, making her giddy. It had been years since she'd felt so alive.

So…you are going?

"What are you thinking about Prudence?"

Prudence jumped. Her older sister Modesty was looking at her from her own bed. She had the covers pulled up to her chin but was staring directly at Prudence instead of sleeping.

"I can see you debating some matter, Prudence. I will tell you firmly that you are not to have any fun without me," Modesty declared in a whisper.

The room they shared was on the back of the house. It had likely been added on as a larder for winter storage, but Prudence and her sisters shared the space now. The wall between the main house and where they were was thick stone.

"Don't think I didn't notice you kept your stockings on tonight," Modesty continued.

Prudence looked over to where their youngest sister was still sleeping, and considered her options. After all, she *did* have her stockings on.

Her guilt must have shown on her face, because Modesty smiled with victory, and sat up, a look of anticipation on her face that matched the excitement brewing inside of Prudence. So she told her sister all about the well, Norla's words to her…and what she was so very tempted to do.

Modesty grinned. "We won't have another chance like this. We'll be stuck inside all winter, because the snow will show every footstep. Can we go?" Modesty asked, jerking her head toward the doorway.

Prudence didn't need any further urging. She was out of bed and getting dressed, as Modesty did the same beside her. Her heart was beating fast in anticipation of something. But what?

She was about to find out.

DUGAN FELT ILL at ease wandering around in the dark.

The Eight Years war might be over because some treaty had

been signed, but that didn't change the fact that the lowlands of Scotland were still a place riddled with men looking for trouble.

Many of them were now desperate, because they'd been "Assured Men"—those who had been aligned with the Scottish nobles who supported the English union of Mary Stuart and Edward VI of England. Aye, a treaty had been signed, but in the lowlands of Scotland, allegiance was a tricky thing.

These days, Dugan didn't sleep soundly at night. Nothing would get in the way of his duty to ensure his clan was protected.

And that was what he was doing tonight, wandering off his own land in hopes of waylaying any raiding parties thinking about venturing into his father's territory. It was a necessary task. Otherwise, the farmers who lived close to the border might be long dead by the time anyone in the Hay stronghold heard about it.

Harvest time was the most dangerous season for farmers— and the most active one, for raiders—because winter supplies often meant the difference between life and a slow death due to starvation.

But no croft in his father's territory would burn—not while he carried a sword.

He and his men had slept in a thicket, waking when darkness fell. Dugan headed toward the Midnight Well. It had been dug a generation before for the Scots who needed to water their horses when so far from their homes.

Dugan grinned. The men who had dug the Midnight Well hadn't limited themselves to the construction of just the well. They'd created a tale to protect the water source. Now the story of the enchantment had been repeated so many times, no one dared to build a house near the landmark. And that left it for men like Dugan.

He paused, his presence concealed in the forest. There was a piece of fruit on the edge of the well, as well as a bucket—both waiting for some lass to come up and test the well's power.

"What are ye waiting on?" Brody, his captain asked.

Dugan pointed at the fruit. A break in the clouds allowed a shimmer of moonlight to illuminate it. "We've arrived on a full moon. It seems there is a lass on her way, intent on testing the enchantment."

Brody grunted. "Matches should be made with an eye on what both bride and groom bring to the union. Any lass who ventures out at night to look into a pail of water is foolish."

Dugan heard a soft crunch, though he didn't see the girl at first. But the clouds seemed to approve of her nighttime venture, clearing away quickly.

The moonlight bathed her, and when she paused to look upward, something stirred inside of him. Dugan didn't really have a grasp of what it was. He'd never felt this way before.

But it was powerful.

And consuming.

It was almost as though there was some unseen rope connecting him to her. He couldn't have taken his eyes off of her if his life depended upon it.

"Why are ye staring at her as though ye've never seen a woman before?" Brody demanded.

"She is different."

"Different?" Brody's voice was edged with exasperation. "What do ye mean by that?"

Dugan merely shrugged. He didn't want to talk. Well, not to Brody. What he wanted to do—what he felt compelled to do— was follow the strange draw he felt tugging him toward the lass.

She walked slowly up to the edge of the well, then reached for the piece of fruit, sparking a new sensation inside of Dugan. This time, he felt the unmistakable flare of raw need.

If she was going to look into the water in search of her soul mate, he wanted to make sure it was his face she saw.

Brody cupped Dugan's shoulder. "Let's go. We do nae need to be found here on the English side of the border. There will be hell to pay."

"I am not planning on being caught," Dugan muttered with a

grin. "I am just going to give that little lass a wee bit of excitement."

It seemed only fair, since she'd captivated him. Dugan started to step forward, but Brody's grip tightened on his shoulder.

"She'll scream," Brody predicted. "And then we'll be running through the forest like a pair of foxes."

"Maybe…"

That was all Dugan said before he eased forward, as if drawn by fate. If only he believed in such things.

There had been a time…

Many years ago, when he'd been very young, he'd been captivated by the hearthside tales of fairies and moonlight magic.

But he was grown now, and such folly had been banished to his memories by the need to be responsible. But this lass stirred something inside him. A thrill of anticipation that he hadn't felt in a long, long time. The feeling was intoxicating. And he suddenly realized how somber and dull his life had become.

All he needed was just a wee taste…

AN APPLE WAS there waiting for her.

Prudence felt breathless when she spied it sitting on the stone edge of the well beside the bucket.

The night air was moving in lazy gusts, which made the dry leaves rustle like running water. When the tree limbs moved, the moonlight filtered through them to illuminate the well.

"It's like a fairy glen," Modesty declared in a hushed tone.

Prudence was struck dumb by its allure.

"Go on," Modesty encouraged her. "Norla left the apple for you. You may place a wager on the fact that I'm going to make sure she leaves something for me next month."

"It's Samhain next month," Prudence reminded her sister.

Modesty's eyes widened with excitement. "Perhaps Norla knows where the bonfires will be. We could go and dance."

Dance? It had been a decade since her father had permitted such merriment. To even think about it was considered a sin by the Puritans. Righteousness must begin inside of her to be sincere, he'd insisted. If they were caught dancing around a bonfire, they might well be tossed into the street for fear their example would corrupt the rest of the family.

"That's too daring," Prudence remarked.

"We could wear masks," Modesty suggested. "As we are so newly arrived, no one will know who we are."

Temptation nibbled on her resolve. The wind blew again, this time carrying a hint of winter that further undermined Prudence's ability to resist the idea of taking the risk, before winter arrived to imprison her.

"Alright," Prudence agreed. "It will be hard to find materials for our masks. You know how mother forbids even a tiny bit of waste."

Yet Prudence was already anticipating the challenge. It was certainly more enticing than breaking chaff from barley stalks.

Modesty nodded with a happy smile on her lips. "Go... See what the moonlight reveals to you tonight."

Silly or not, Prudence walked the last few steps and reached out for the apple. It was smooth and hard, just big enough to fill her hand. She lifted it to her lips and took a bite.

The sweet and tart taste burst through her mouth. She crunched the flesh of the fruit between her teeth and swallowed, before taking another bite, and then a few more, until only the core remained. As she swallowed the last bite, she leaned over the bucket with her eyes closed and her mind empty.

The wind roared behind her. It chilled her lips where they were wet from the juice. She concentrated on keeping her mind blank, trying to feel as though she was encased inside a dark cloud. When she opened her eyes again, she'd emerge from that darkness, and look at what had been hidden from her. Prudence smiled and took a deep breath because her heart was thumping hard, then she opened her eyes.

And looked into the eyes of a man reflected in the water.

Prudence blinked, completely astonished. Yet the image was still there when she opened her eyes again.

How could such a thing be?

She didn't bother to cover her gaping mouth with her hand. Her attention was riveted on the face, her mind trying to absorb every detail.

Who was he?

While she stared at the reflection, the wind blew, and it carried the soft sound of a man's chuckle to her ears. Prudence recoiled, straightening up. She hopped back a pace and bumped into someone behind her.

"God's wounds!" The less than polite words simply flew out of her mouth. Prudence whirled around and felt her eyes go wide, because he was in fact standing behind her.

"I hope ye are not too disappointed to discover I am not an incarnation of the night fairy, lass." He reached up to tug on the corner of her knitted bonnet.

She had to lift her chin in order to meet his gaze, for he was so much taller than she was. The moonlight was filtering through the leaves that weren't ready to fall just yet.

All she saw were shadows.

But he was there, as large and as real as she herself was.

Unless she was dreaming…

No, the sweet taste of the apple still filled her mouth. Her lips were cold from the wind, and whoever he was, his kilt fluttered with the breeze.

She had no idea how long they stood there, for it felt like she'd stepped inside a single moment of time, and once there, she'd become frozen inside the enchantment.

Then he moved, bursting the bubble around them. He held his hand up in front of her, his palm facing upward in a silent invitation.

Did she dare to place her hand into his?

Her breath froze in her lungs as Prudence lifted her hand. She couldn't resist. Their gazes locked. His flesh was warm when she placed her hand in his.

He was no enchantment…

She gasped and Modesty gasped louder.

"Prudence…." her sister called out to her.

He released her hand almost in the same moment that her sister spoke. The man flashed her a wide smile, then, a single breath later, he turned, and melted into the darkness, as though he'd never been there at all.

Yet he had.

Prudence blinked.

He had been there!

That single touch had her skin tingling. Never before had she ever imagined that her skin might be so sensitive.

And somehow, she knew that nothing was ever going to be the same again.

Hay Land

"DUGAN? CAN I ride with ye tonight?" Rohan asked earnestly from where he was standing near the stable door.

Dugan gave his younger half-brother his full attention. At twelve winters, Rohan was lanky, but tall. He watched the men making ready to ride, excitement shining in his young eyes. Dugan recalled being just as eager in his youth. Now though, Dugan would have to be the one to deny the lad for his own good.

"Ye know I cannae take ye out without permission," Dugan said.

Rohan jutted out his chin. "I am a Hay! The next laird. Why should I need a woman's permission to ride out and defend me own land?"

"Because she is yer lady mother," Dugan stated firmly. "And

mistress of this stronghold."

"All she does is keep me with my tutors." Rohan kicked a cloud of dirt. "The retainers will never respect me if I don't ride with them like you do."

"Ye'll be grown soon enough Rohan." Dugan tried to sound encouraging. "Off with ye now. Back to the hall. The cook will be laying down the supper."

Rohan wasn't interested in being obedient, but Dugan looked past him, locking gazes with the stable master. The man dusted off his hands and came toward Rohan.

"Ye see?" Rohan whined. "The men respect you."

"Come along, young master," the stable master said softly.

Rohan went along reluctantly. Brody let out a grunt. "That scamp doesn't realize what trouble would rain down upon us if we gave in and took him out."

There were answering chuckles from the other Hay retainers.

"Lady Hay would have me balls for sure," Dugan agreed.

"She'd have yer balls all right, but only because she does nae want ye to have any descendants to compete with her son," Brody grumbled.

The good-natured mood vanished instantly. Dugan watched the faces around him tighten.

"I am content with me place," Dugan stated quietly. "And pleased to know the next laird will be very well educated."

The men around him nodded with approval. Dugan returned to checking the saddle on his horse. There was a tiny bit of moisture on his forehead, and he mopped it away quickly.

Diplomacy always tested him. Truthfully, he much preferred being direct, but when it came to the matter of just who would be the next laird of the Hay, he needed to make sure he didn't say anything that might make the men around him consider anyone other than Rohan.

Such a topic could rip the clan apart.

Dugan had no stomach for a legacy begun in the spilt blood of his kin. His horse shook its head, eager to leave the stable. Aye, he agreed with his mount. Better to be in the saddle and away from the topic of power. Lady Hay was welcome to it.

"We've duty to see to," Dugan said, happy to change the subject. "The harvest is in. There will no doubt be villains intent on pilfering."

Dugan led his horse out of the stable, with his men following behind him. The week before the full moon was a time of dark nights—the perfect time for raids.

⇶⇷

LAIRD HAY WATCHED from a tower as Dugan and his men rode out of the stronghold. His lips curved into a satisfied smile.

"Father?" Rohan appeared in the doorway of Cormac's study.

Cormac turned toward his youngest son. Rohan's expression was tight with determination.

"Will you allow me to go riding with Dugan?" Rohan asked, launching straight into what he wanted.

"Yer brother is off to safeguard our land," Cormac answered. "It is not a place for a half-grown youth. Mind yer lady mother, Rohan."

Rohan's forehead furrowed with frustration.

"My lady mother forbids me to call Dugan brother because he is a bastard."

"Dugan is a man who just rode out of this stronghold into the uncertain night to protect our land with his blood if necessary," Cormac growled.

"Yet mother says I must make sure everyone remembers that Dugan is a bastard," Rohan argued.

Cormac drew in a deep breath. "Does she now?"

Rohan nodded firmly.

Cormac felt his temper flaring, but he calmed it. When it came to his lady wife, he needed to be clear-headed. His wife was a very cunning adversary, one who was using all of her wits to maneuver her son into position. But when it came to the clan, Cormac was practical enough to know that men only followed men.

Respect had to be earned through deeds, not words.

DUGAN SAW HER face in his dreams every night.

By the time that the moon was full later that week, he should have been too tired to think of anything but returning to the Hay stronghold—and his bed—after several nights of sleeping on the ground.

Yet her face refused to be banished from his thoughts. He'd never been so tempted by something before. He found himself looking south, toward the borderlands.

"It's Samhain, lads," Dugan said, giving in to his need to see the lass once more. "I've a mind to find a bonfire tonight."

Just one last time...

"Ye're mad, to think of going to see that lass again," Brody said, obviously knowing what was on Dugan's mind.

Dugan smiled at his friend, before slapping him on the shoulder. "Just a wee bit of harvest time fun. Fairly earned, I'd say."

Dugan watched as his friend, and captain, mulled over the facts. Brody was weakening.

"Come now Brody," Dugan teased his friend. "It's Samhain."

"I know it. But I am telling ye...ye are playing with fire when it comes to this lass," Brody said, pressing his opinion. "Ye want to see her, and once ye do, ye'll want to do it again."

Dugan locked gazes with his man. "Do nae begrudge me a bit of harvest celebration. Winter will be here shortly enough, keeping me far away from the lass."

Finally, Brody cracked. "She is a pretty thing," he admitted. "I suppose if a man is going to get his fingers singed...she would be a fine enough flame to reach for." Then Brody pointed at him. "But ye are toying with fire lad." He crossed his arms over his chest.

"I seek merriment and misrule on the hillsides. Stay here and sleep with the old men if ye like," Dugan taunted.

His decision made, Dugan felt freer, as if he'd cast off a chain that had kept him bound. There were only a few precious hours between him and the dawn, which would see the little lass hurrying back to her home.

He intended to make the most of them.

"Hold up," Brody called out. "I'm coming along with ye."

Dugan grinned. Brody, the man his laird father had assigned to him as companion and captain, was as close to a brother as he had. Like Dugan, Brody had been born on the wrong side of the bedding, and together, the two of them made a fine pair of black sheep in the Hay clan.

And a black sheep couldn't be made white. So there was no point in him tempering his impulses.

None at all.

CHAPTER TWO

England

ER KNEES ACHED.

That was a bit surprising, for Prudence was quite accustomed to the long prayer sessions her father insisted upon. Although 'enjoyed' was likely a better choice of words, for her father was truly devoted.

Still, tonight, her sire was particularly zealous in his evening prayers.

And she dared not move.

Anticipation for the revels tonight was bubbling up inside of her. Every second felt interminable, as her mind teased her with memories of the Samhains she'd celebrated before her father had become a Puritan. Back then, there had been dancing, feasting, and cider. And with luck, tonight, she'd have a chance to experience all that again!

You cannot make the sun move faster…

Her sister elbowed her—she'd missed her part in the end of the evening prayer. Her heart thumped hard. She dreaded seeing the expression on her father's face when she opened her eyes. There was nothing for it, of course. So she took a little breath and opened her eyes, ready to accept her fate.

"You were deep in prayer tonight daughter," her father said.

Prudence could only stare back at him. She didn't want to be dishonest, but… She nodded in agreement.

Thankfully, her father appeared satisfied. He turned to offer his wife his hand. Prudence waited until he'd helped her mother off her knees, before she herself stood.

There was a very strict order in the house.

Her father and mother came first, then her brothers, and finally the daughters of the family. They all filed into the dining room for their meal.

The aroma of supper filled the air.

She studied the simple meal. Puritans believed that keeping life simple was a way of following Christ's example while he had been on earth. Tonight, the fare was extremely bland, as if to prove that her family had abandoned the excesses that other faiths would be indulging in on Samhain.

"There is great reward in avoiding the vice of abundance," her father said softly.

Prudence didn't lament the plainness of the meal. In fact, tonight, she was grateful, very aware that they wouldn't be on the borderlands if they had not been Puritans. And in the borderlands, anything was possible…

These lands between Scotland and England were still wild. In this place, she might escape into the hills and enjoy a little freedom tonight, before the winter forced her to remain inside.

You mean, you might see the man from the well again…

She wouldn't deny that he was all she could think of.

"Remember to stuff up your ears tonight," her mother said as Prudence and her sisters rose from the table. "There will be wickedness carried on the wind from those partaking of pagan rituals. I have put wool in your room."

"Yes, Mother," Modesty said, answering for them all.

Walking slowly back to her room had never been so difficult before. She was driven by the urge to rush as her mind filled with all the merriment ahead of her. Just as their mother had said, a small bundle of newly carded wool sat on the end of one of the beds.

Prudence and Modesty quickly tore at the bedding, pushing

and tugging on it, making it appear as if they were under the covers, asleep.

"Perhaps we should stay in," her youngest sister, Temperance suggested. Modesty had invited the girl to go with them, but clearly, Temperance was worried about being caught.

"Stay if you like," Modesty answered. "But I am going."

"As am I," Prudence added.

"Are you not afeared of wickedness?" Temperance asked with wide eyes.

Modesty shared a look with Prudence before she smiled at their youngest sister.

"I remember when your name was Anne," Modesty said.

Temperance smiled. "I liked the name Anne."

"Of course you did," Prudence added. "I much preferred being called Braylin to Prudence."

The light cast by their little tin lantern illuminated the girl. She started to smile, then froze, her lips pressed into a hard line. "Father is firmly resolute that Puritanism will benefit our immortal souls," she stated. "Our brothers are proof that God is pleased with our new faith." Then she sighed in resignation. "We should stay in tonight…stuff up our ears and avoid wickedness. As mother says, to even know the way of wickedness, is to awaken unrest inside a woman."

Wickedness had already been awakened inside of her…

Prudence realized it was true and yet, she had no desire to temper her impulses. In truth, she craved some adventure, feeling as if she might miss out on her own life if she didn't break through the constraints put upon her.

Modesty leaned close to Temperance. "Do as you please, but you shall keep your lips sealed on the matter of what we are doing. No carrying tales."

"But—"

"No arguments," Modesty insisted. "There has been dancing on the hillsides every Samhain for too many years to count. Yet we are all still here in spite of it."

Temperance opened her mouth, as if to argue, then shut it without speaking.

Prudence smiled, feeling like a horse who had been locked inside the barn far too long. All hints of hesitation were gone.

The moors awaited.

And who knew what else?

PRUDENCE AND MODESTY weren't the only ones out in the darkness.

In the time between sunset and moonrise, they made their way across the newly harvested fields. The stocks were cut and dried now, which meant their steps made crunching and brushing sounds.

A shiver touched her nape, but Prudence only smiled. It was Samhain after all. The one night of the year when the worlds of the living and the dead were separated by the thinnest of veils. Just like the seasons of harvest and winter. One was complete abundance, the other, barren.

She wasn't going to think of winter tonight.

Tonight, she'd be Braylin once more.

Ahead of them, they caught the twinkle of the bonfire beckoning to them in the darkness. A dancing spot of orange and yellow in the seemingly endless abyss of blackness.

So welcoming...

It drew them out of the forest, up toward the top of a ridge. By the time they arrived, the fire was huge. Obviously, nobody worried about how much wood was being burnt.

Tonight was about abundance.

A crowd was gathering. In the darkness, she could see a group of men and women cast in the shadows of the flames.

"Put your mask on," Modesty reminded her.

Prudence stopped and pulled out the simple mask she'd hidden inside her partlet. She had searched hard to find enough bits of fabric to complete it, for there was very little material wasted in their meager household. In the end, she'd resorted to utilizing a few leaves to complete it.

Yet she discovered it was worth the effort, because once she tied the mask into place, a sense of freedom enveloped her.

At last.

Prudence hadn't realized how tight she'd been drawn until it was all released. Now, she might enjoy the crisp air on her cheeks and the way the fire warmed her nose before it became chilled. All around them, there was feasting. Everyone had brought something to share. She and her sister quickly sat down on a length of wool fabric which served as a modest table to enjoy the offerings.

"We need a Lord of Misrule!" someone called out.

"Yes!"

"Aye!"

Clapping began as a few men stumbled into the circle closest to the fire. One was drinking from his mug, cider dripping down his beard. He sent those watching a huge smile and tipped his mug again.

The crowd laughed, encouraging his display of gluttony.

The next man danced nimbly into the center of the clearing. Around them, those playing music began to increase the tempo until he fell over his own feet. There was a puff of dirt when he landed, and he raised his arms up. The crowd rewarded him with applause and cheers.

"If ye want to be led astray and engulfed in debauchery, what ye need is…a Laird of Misrule!"

There was a gasp as the newcomer strode out into the center of the firelight. His knees were bare, the bottom of his kilt allowing everyone to see them. Unlike the others, he strode purposely forward and planted himself firmly in front of them.

Prudence felt her body tense.

It was him. The man she'd seen in the well.

Her belly twisted. She set aside the barely tasted cider in her hand, not wanting her wits to be dulled even a bit.

For certain, this man intoxicated her simply by being near.

The rest of the assembled people were happily looking at the newcomer. They craved a celebration that would live in their memories for the length of the cold months ahead. The Scot raised his massive arms up and roared.

There were squeals and then louder laughter than before.

"What ye really need…." the man said, "is a wild…*Scottish* Laird of Misrule!"

Everyone beat their hands together. A man wearing a woman's dress came up to him, bestowing a crown made of rams' horns, then danced around to everyone's delight.

The newly crowned Laird of Misrule nodded. "This one looks like her father, sure enough!" he laughed.

The man in the dress opened his mouth in feigned surprise. The Scot lifted his foot to give him a playful kick on the backside. "I think I'll be looking elsewhere for my consort, thank ye."

Another man dressed as a woman went up to the Scot, making a mockery of courtly manners as he delivered a mug of ale to the Laird of Misrule.

"Not this one either," the Scot shouted, waving his hands in dismissal. He scanned the crowd and locked gazes with her. "I crave that one."

Prudence's eyes went wide.

Everyone turned to see where their Laird of Misrule was pointing.

Modesty let out a squeak and dove down to flatten herself against the ground, leaving Prudence in sight and the easiest to claim. Men came at her, hooking her arms and legs and lifted her up as though she weighed no more than a child.

The musicians changed to a lively tune often played during weddings.

"Wait…wait," the women cried out. "A bride has to let her hair down!"

Prudence was suddenly on her feet as fingers dug into the

pins that held her linen cap in place.

Except for her family, no one had ever seen her hair ….

Still, the cap was stripped away, and her long hair freed from the coil she had pinned to the back of her head. Someone was combing it out, as someone else found the ribbons which held her partlet closed beneath her arms. The sturdy piece of wool which covered the square neckline of her dress was taken away, offering a look at the top swells of her breasts.

"Oh really…I should not…" she protested.

It's why you came…isn't it? To be daring and bold…to be Braylin…

She couldn't deny what her inner voice asked. She was guilty of courting this very thing—and it was happening—and yet, she didn't feel guilty at all, but exhilarated and more alive than she had ever been.

Would he be pleased with her?

The group around her was enjoying the moment hugely. They laughed as they turned her around and presented her to their chosen Laird of Misrule.

"Your consort, Laird!"

As they delivered Prudence to him, the merrymakers prostrated themselves in reverence, making a mocking imitation of being the subjects before the laird and his lady. Around them, music filled the air.

His mask didn't cover the bottom of his face. She held her breath, waiting to see what he thought of her, now that her cap and partlet were gone.

Did he think she was pretty? She couldn't tell. But she liked the way he looked at her. There wasn't a hint of meekness about him, and she found herself wanting to act just as bold. She lifted her chin so that their gazes locked. "We meet again," she muttered in a husky tone which surprised her. She was rather certain she had never sounded so daring before.

In the darkness, Prudence couldn't see the color of his eyes, but the mocking smile on his face grew wider when she spoke.

He offered his hand to her.

Just as he had before…

"Are ye brave enough to take my hand tonight lass?" His tone was deep, beckoning to her with a hint of promise.

There would only be this night.

Perhaps. But she hadn't imagined the number of times she'd awakened in the dark hours of the night, thinking about that moment at the well.

She wasn't going to waste this opportunity. Tomorrow would be soon enough for her to become Prudence once more.

"I am," Prudence answered smoothly as she placed her hand in his.

CHAPTER THREE

PRUDENCE THOUGHT HER memory had exaggerated the way she'd felt when she'd first put her hand into his.

Real life simply wasn't so very intense…

Yet now that they were touching again, something rippled up her arm—a sensation which raised gooseflesh. She felt as if her breath had frozen in her chest, and that she was suspended between heartbeats. The intensity of it caught her completely off guard.

His eyes narrowed as she felt him close his fingers around hers. Her breath caught. The touch of his skin, the firmness of his grasp… She knew this night would be forever branded in her mind…and that she'd recall the feeling of his flesh against hers until she drew her very last breath.

Something glittered in his eyes before he gently tugged her forward. Around them, people danced, and the music played. Yet all Prudence saw was him, and the way he seemed to be studying her, as if he was equally fascinated with her.

Still, it was likely just her vanity talking. Disappointment raked it claws through her, for she truly wanted to believe she was capable of captivating him. But that would be folly.

"Are you pleased with your bride?" someone demanded.

The fingers around hers tightened.

"I am…enchanted!" he bellowed.

Cheers rose up around them and for just that moment, Prudence allowed herself to believe his words. Even if it was folly, it was the reason she'd come tonight.

Perhaps that was what they truly shared—the desire to let the conflict between their two countries fall away into nothingness, while they enjoyed a taste of what would be considered forbidden in the morning.

Tonight, Scot and English would dance together.

A huge ring of people swayed around the fire, their hands clasped, the tempo of the music driving their pace. The flames of the fire rose into the dark sky—little ruby sparks floated even higher before they died. The pounding of so many feet raised the scent of moist earth as they trampled down the dried grass beneath their dancing. The fire popped and the flames warmed her cheeks.

It was pagan and yet so very natural, making her feel as if she was answering some instinct that was centered in the very core of her bones. She felt a need to celebrate life, to simply shout with it.

Prudence had never felt so very alive.

Her heart pounded inside her chest, as sweat trickled down the sides of her face. She was grateful to be free of her partlet now, for she was far too warm for the garment. All of her clothing suddenly felt like ropes, binding her true nature. Having her hair flowing in the night breeze was more enjoyable than anything she'd ever felt.

Freedom….it was so wonderful!

"Enough!" the laird called out. "I must feed my bride!"

He pulled them away from the ring of dancers, but didn't release her hand. Instead, he settled it upon his forearm, as if they were strolling through a market fair, their union accepted by one and all.

She'd never been so close to a man before. And she liked it.

She suddenly realized how her cheeks were stinging with a blush.

And how excited she was to feel the burn.

She didn't have to wonder what her mother would think.

'Modesty protects you from your baser instincts. Forget not that the

seeds of Eve are inside you. Inattention to your behavior will see them awakened and then, you will fall prey to wicked intentions.'

Somehow, Prudence had never grasped just how nice it might feel to have...things inside her awakened. Yes, her cheeks stung, yet it felt like her blood was racing through her veins, making her feel lightheaded.

And she liked it.

Was that truly so terrible? To enjoy being alive?

She looked at her companion. He was huge, with solid looking shoulders and forearms cut with defined muscles.

"What is yer name, lass?"

Of course, he'd noticed her looking at him.

Gaping, you mean...

Her mouth wasn't quite hanging open, but it had to be obvious that she was dumbstruck. When she didn't answer, he frowned and moved closer to her.

"Is it yer plan to deny me yer name?" He lifted a mug of cider to his lips and drank from it, continuing to stare at her over the rim of the mug. "I am called Dugan."

Gaelic...

He opened his hand toward her, clearly expecting her to respond in kind.

"Prudence," she replied.

He lowered the mug to the ground and tilted his head slightly to one side. "Are ye saying ye feel it would be prudent not to share yer name with me?"

Her mother would surely think it a wise course of action.

Your mother would be aghast to know you are here and not sleeping with your ears full of wool...

She shook her head. "My name is Prudence."

He frowned and shook his head.

"Now who would name such a fetching lass something like that?" he exclaimed incredulously.

She had to admit, she liked him even more just for his reaction to her name. Yet she squirmed, feeling like she should explain.

"My father had three daughters, but he longed for sons. Hence, he embraced the reform…I have three brothers now," she rambled. "Since the Lord granted my father his desired sons, my sire renamed me and my sisters after virtues he believed we should devote ourselves to."

He made a 'humph' sound before taking another drink from his cider. He stopped before putting the cup down.

"It sounds as though ye need this a wee bit more than I do," Dugan said, offering the mug to her.

It was a simple earthenware vessel that was cool against her palms. The aroma of the cider filled her senses as she lifted it to her lips. Sweet apples and spices. She inhaled, wanting to savor the forbidden moment completely. The brew hit her tongue, awakening tastebuds which had been lulled into deep slumber by the dull offerings she was used to. She took a second, longer sip, before managing to make herself lower the mug.

Dugan was grinning at her.

"What was yer other name?" he asked.

"Other name?" Prudence asked, because she couldn't seem to think.

"Aye," he said, placing the mug down, then reaching for some cheese. "Before yer father became a…how is it said in England? Puritan?"

She nodded. "Yes, we're Puritans now. As such, we are not welcome by our new queen Mary."

He cocked his head to one side.

"I am the Laird of Misrule, lass… 'Tis only fair to warn ye that I will be merciless in my quest to learn yer name." He raised his hands up, his fingers curled. "Shall I tickle ye until ye submit to me?"

"You will do no such thing!" She meant to sound outraged, but the unmistakable breathlessness in her voice surprised her.

Was that really her?

One of his dark eyebrows rose above the edge of his mask.

"Ye have exposed yer weakness lass…."

He wiggled his fingers again, making a good show of coming at her. Evading him was rather simple. Of course, she realized he might have captured her if it had been his true intention, but instead, he lunged playfully at her, and she jumped away easily.

Dugan ended up poised on all fours as he contemplated her.

There was suddenly a hoot. Those watching began to add their suggestions to the chase.

"After her Laird!"

"Claim yer prize!"

"Take what you like!"

The jests were becoming more suggestive, eroding her enjoyment. She frowned, looking around for her sister.

Dugan lost his playful expression and suddenly rose to his feet.

"I command ye all…to be chickens! Ye men, crow loudly to impress the hens!"

Most of the people dancing were well on their way to the bottom of their third cup of cider, and immediately started grinning like besotted fools, hooting at the command their Laird of Misrule had given them. The musicians changed to a comic song and then the lot of them returned to dancing, flapping their arms while the men crowed.

Modesty was suddenly by her side. She put Prudence's cap back on top of her head as though it might protect her like a helmet and gathered up Prudence's flowing hair and tucked it back up. Then she slipped Prudence's partlet back on.

Dugan returned to his seat. "Come back here now. That lot out there is too deep into their mugs for ye to be joining them anymore. Best to remain by my side."

Prudence realized that while Dugan was very good at appearing intoxicated, his stare was solid.

"Yer sister should sit here as yer attendant," Dugan continued. "As any proper queen consort would have."

The rising level of lewdness in the crowd's even more boisterous songs was like sand in an hourglass, counting down the time until she would have to leave.

Prudence realized she truly did not want this night to end. Not just yet. She sat back down, and Dugan resumed eating. There was a feast in front of them—meat, cheese, fruit. Prudence looked at it, clasping her hands together as she realized she could indulge freely, without any Puritan guilt.

"Ye may have all ye like lass," Dugan told her.

"Yes, and yet, no. For my belly will burst if I am too much of a glutton," she replied.

"Ummm," he muttered. "I suppose ye have a valid point there."

He reached for the fruit, picking it up and raising it in the air so it caught the firelight. Prudence shivered as memory and the night around her seemed to combine into a type of intoxication which stemmed directly from being near him. Normal things, such as eating became magical when she did them with him.

He pulled a knife from the top of his boot and sliced the apple in half and then into quarters.

"Here lass," he said, handing two of the sections to her. "Let us enjoy the harvest bounty together. The cheese will last through the winter."

"Kiss yer bride!" someone yelled.

Prudence felt her heart stop. Dugan's expression tightened. He looked at the group around the fire.

"I am a laird, no a lack-wit!" Dugan informed them all. "A lady of such caliber must be wooed gently. Dare I even say...nobly."

The merrymakers accepted Dugan's explanation without protest, raising their tankards high before resuming their celebration.

"Eat up lass," Dugan muttered. "For it is almost time for ye and yer sister to depart. Too much drink robs good souls of their senses. It's best to not be here where mistakes can be made."

Prudence suddenly realized Dugan was not alone. There

were several other Scots about. They were quiet and very serious, with each man taking a position where he might keep watch in a different direction. Though they were enjoying the food, not a single one had a mug in their hand. She caught the one nearest to them share a warning look with her Laird of Misrule.

Dugan rose in a fluid, powerful motion. "Come lasses," he said, offering a hand to Prudence. Another of his men was there to help Modesty to her feet. "It is time to depart."

There was lament in his voice. Yet it was nothing compared to the regret Prudence felt as Modesty reached out to clasp her upper arm.

But of course she should go…

Around the fire, the amount of drink consumed was leading to more displays of lewdness. One man grabbed at a woman, and she squealed in delight, whirling around to smile encouragingly at him. Prudence wasn't the only one being quietly led away into the darkness.

Yet she was with a Scot.

Still, Dugan was her protector—the exact opposite of what she'd always been told to expect from a Scotsman.

He still held her hand, pulling her gently behind him. The night closed around them, like a cloak. The feeling of his fingers clasping hers made her feel warm, hot even, and though she shivered, it wasn't from the cold.

It was strange the way darkness made every sound more intense. Without her sight, Prudence heard their footsteps more keenly, the crunching sounds of dry plants being crushed beneath their shoes. The wind was gusting too. It blew the tree limbs against one another, and the half dry leaves rattled.

In the light of day, the sounds were innocent enough.

Encased in darkness, her mind wanted to assign specters and demons to the sounds.

But the warm grip on her hand seemed to be all the protection she needed. The strength in his grip banished her fear, keeping it away as they walked.

She heard the sound of a horse.

A few more paces, and suddenly, the horses were in sight, held steady by a couple of younger Scots.

Dugan mounted easily, his kilt flipping up to grant her a glimpse of his powerful thigh before he settled quite confidently on the back of a huge beast.

"Come lass." He offered her his hand. "I'll see ye safely to yer home."

"We walked," Modesty stated beside her.

"The fields ye crossed are now inhabited by a fair number of couples who would no take kindly to an interruption," Dugan informed them. "Take my hand lass. It is best."

Though his tone was gentle, there was a solid core which warned her he wasn't going to settle for anything less than her submission.

It felt natural to put her hand in his once more.

Clearly, she had fallen under the spell of the moon, for it was madness to trust someone she barely knew.

But none of that seemed to matter as she was lifted and sat in front of him. His arms were around her as he held onto the reins of the horse. She heard her sister gasp and turned her head to see the burly Scot who had stood near Dugan depositing Modesty on the back of another horse before he mounted behind her.

"Brody is trustworthy," Dugan assured her. "Yer sister will come to no harm with him."

If he wasn't, she and her sister would be in quite a bit of trouble because they were surrounded by Scots.

The sound of the horses seemed loud as they set off, with Modesty pointing in the direction of their home. The distance was covered quickly, the horses eager to be in motion.

A few minutes later, Dugan pulled his steed to a stop while still in the trees. He slid off his horse, then reached up to lift her off the back of the animal.

Once she was firmly on the ground again, Dugan caught her hand and raised it up to his lips, pressing a kiss against the back of it. Another little ripple skated along her arm. Moonlight filtered through the tree limbs and for a moment, she caught a glimpse of the grin on his face.

"Farewell to ye lass. I confess, I lament our parting, but I am on the wrong side of the border." Dugan explained.

He'd taken a great risk to meet her…twice.

She wanted to ask him why, or anything to put off his departure for just a bit longer, but Modesty came up beside her.

The sand in the hourglass had run dry.

Dugan mounted his horse with a powerful movement. He was so very suited to the midnight ride, appearing to be one with the darkness and strong enough to face anything which might befall him.

"Back to yer maiden's bed lass." Dugan made a motion with his hand. "Ye have tempted me quite enough."

Tempted him?

Did she have the power to do such a thing? For her dress was plain and she wore no adornments in her hair. Didn't one need to be flashy to tempt a man?

Prudence pondered that idea as her cheeks heated. Modesty tugged her back toward the small manor house where they lived. It was quiet and dark, and so very dull now that she had something to compare it to.

But adventures had to come to an end. And it was best that it happen before they became misadventures.

Even though a part of her was dying inside.

"LEAVE HER LAD. Ye ken 'tis best."

Brody was the voice of reason.

At least, he was attempting to be.

His steed was impatient to be off as well, side-stepping when Dugan hesitated to turn the horse to the north.

Braylin and her sister were just shadows in the dark now. Dugan watched as they crept toward the house and then entered one of the doorways in the back of the kitchen.

Brody gave a snort. "Little wonder we've never seen them before. Only a newly arrived family would put their daughters in a room on the backside of the hearth."

Dugan knew the house.

He and his men had sheltered inside it more than once when it had been closed up.

"I do nae suppose her parents would take too kindly to me advising them of the mistake they are making in letting their daughters sleep where they do," Dugan remarked dryly.

"That would be a wager ye'd win for certain," Brody answered with a snort.

Which meant he had to leave things as they were. To be sure, it was by far not the first time Dugan had faced riding away from a matter which he knew needed intervention. Daughters should be above stairs, where the men of the house could shield them from raiders.

They'd come from the city, where a cry for help might be heard. But not out here.

He still smelled her hair…

There was something about her that bewitched him. Part of him wanted to dismiss it as nothing more than the effects of cider and dancing. Yet there was another part of him that was bemused to discover himself so enthralled with her after such a short encounter.

No one had ever accused him of being a romantic.

And that was because he wasn't.

Aye, yet he was tempted to ask her to leave with him…

But there was a border between them and the matter of faith. Her father would never agree to the match, any more than Braylin would find a warm welcome back on Hay land.

Scot and English, there were too many conflicts between their countries for them to find harmony. It was a cruel twist of fate to discover himself so stirred by her. The kindest thing he could do would be to never see her again.

Dugan turned his horse around and pressed his knees into the animal's sides to start it moving. His horse was happy to be heading north, and picked up speed, while Dugan felt the parting keenly.

It was for the best.

Yet it felt worse than anything ever had.

CHAPTER FOUR

PRUDENCE DREAMED OF Dugan.

When she woke, her cheeks were still warm. She still couldn't believe she and Modesty had had the nerve to sneak out and go to the bonfire. The bonfire where she'd spent time with Dugan…

He was a Scot. Yet he was clean shaven, something which did not fit with the tales she'd heard of the Scots and their savage ways.

His man Brody had a beard though.

However, Brody's beard wasn't unkept or greasy. And both men smelled good—something that could not be said of many of the members of the congregation with whom they sometimes attended services. There was more than one Puritan who believed bathing was a vanity and soap doubly so.

She looked down and saw her mask on the floor beside her bed.

Prudence gasped, and reached down to swipe it off the floor before it might be discovered. She folded it and pushed it into her bodice before putting her partlet on and tying it securely in place. She was covered from neck to ankle now.

She should burn the mask. Such would be the safest course of action.

Yet she discovered herself loathe to do so.

It was a memento.

A treasure…

Something that would help her to smile in the long, dark days of winter when there would be naught but piety and devotion.

Of course, she realized she was fortunate to have her family with her. It was a blessing many did not have. Even knowing that didn't stop her from thinking of the music from the night before with a blissful smile on her lips.

How had that tune gone? If she concentrated, she could recall the notes...and the tempo...

"Prudence? I have called you four times at least..." Her mother appeared in the bedroom, making Prudence jump.

Her mother frowned at her. "You are still brushing your hair out? It is fully past first light."

"Forgive me," Prudence answered quickly. Wasting sunlight was never a good thing. And with winter arriving, there would be plenty of dark night hours in which to ponder her thoughts.

"Finish up," her mother instructed in a mild tone. "Best to get to the washing, for I expect it's as warm as it is likely to be today."

Which meant she should expect the water to be freezing.

Prudence could already feel her fingers protesting but she hurried to braid and secure her hair because she'd rather suffer stiff fingers than have her father decide that bathing and washing were a vanity. She could live without luxuries well enough. But smelling was truly something she doubted she could ignore.

Can you live without seeing Dugan again?

Prudence froze as the thought came to mind.

And she couldn't push the thought aside. In fact, the Scotsman's face suddenly filled her mind as clearly as though he was standing in front of her.

Something had awakened inside her.

Doing her best to forget, Prudence pulled her linen cap down and over her hair with a firm tug. Her fascination was giving way to irritation—there was no future in her recollections. Except to torment her with what could never be hers.

And the daylight was wasting!

Hay castle

ALICE SINCLAIR ENJOYED her position as lady of the Hay clan.

And truly, she had every right to, for it had taken careful planning and perseverance to secure her position.

Suddenly, a movement caught her eye. Alice shifted her gaze to the side in time to catch the maid who stood there fingering her apron.

Alice considered just what to do with the girl. She was her husband's spy, of course.

But a young retainer named Cray walked past the hearth just then. He paused and placed his hand on the mantel, staring into the fire for a moment. He left a moment later, heading for the place where Alice had previously instructed him to meet her when he had information to pass along.

"Erin," Alice said to the maid. "I crave some marzipan."

The girl lowered herself into a curtsey before she headed off, her pace brisk, betraying how happy she was to have a reason to leave the hall. She'd dawdle for certain, giving Alice plenty of time to meet with the retainer.

Alice waited until the girl disappeared behind the opening in the wall which connected the great hall to the passageway which ran to the kitchens. The moment Erin was gone, Alice rose and went out another doorway, this one leading to the stairwell which wound its way up into the keep at the far north end of the hall.

Cray would never use the stairs, for her private apartments were on the top floor. Alice had not worked so very hard to become lady of the manor only to be accused of infidelity.

Lucky for her, there was a secret door that led into a store-room beneath the ground floor—an escape tunnel built by one of the past lairds. Now, Alice made good use of it. She found Cray waiting for her in what had once been a ladies' solar. Now it was the lowest level of the keep and a storeroom.

"Where did my husband's bastard go last night?" Alice asked, wasting no time in getting to the subject which most concerned her.

Dugan was illegitimate, but he was still a son, and a grown one. His less than proper entrance into the world might well be overlooked if Laird Hay died before Alice's own son came to his maturity. And that was something Alice would not allow to happen.

"He went to a Samhain celebration on the English side of the border ma'am," Cray reported dully.

Alice made a motion with her hand for Cray to continue. The retainer thought for a moment, not accustomed to being allowed to freely speak to her.

"He…he was crowned the Laird of Misrule and drank and ate his fill…." Cray continued.

Alice was making a slow circle around the room while she listened.

"Oh…and there was a young miss presented to him…as a consort of sorts."

Alice turned so quickly, her skirts spun up and away from her ankles. "Did they consummate the union?"

Cray shook his head. "She was a proper lass. Linen cap and covered up to her chin. The merrymakers stripped her down a bit, startling the lass, but Dugan was a fine, honorable man about it all. Ye may be proud of his behavior. He took her on home when things started becoming too heated."

"So they were alone," Alice said, picking up on that part of the tale.

"No precisely," Cray argued. "Ye ken Brody and the others never leave Dugan on his own. The laird would have their hides."

"Yes, I know it very well," Lady Alice confirmed.

And there was the difficulty. Her husband had a deep affection for his firstborn son. So did a great number of the Hay retainers. Unfortunately, Alice's own son was barely ten winters old. His position would never hold up against Dugan if the clan needed new leadership. In Scotland, a child could never be laird.

And that was why Dugan had to be watched.

Alice circled the room, pacing while Cray held his tongue and waited.

"Go and find out about the girl," Alice decided. "I want to know everything about her, including her family status."

Cray looked at her strangely, obviously not understanding what Alice was asking.

Of course, he didn't. He was a young man who'd earned his rank through his strength and obedience. As a woman, she had to employ her wits. Making sure Dugan couldn't become laird was one of the most important duties she had to complete, if her own son was to eventually rise to power.

The retainer tugged on the corner of his cap before he carefully left the room, his lack of enthusiasm for the task she'd given him pronounced.

It might come to nothing. However, Dugan was an honorable man, which was another thing which concerned Alice. If he were lecherous or a drunkard or arrogant, she would rest much easier at night. Diligence was the only weapon she had against her husband's bastard. She had to press forward and refuse to give up. Every man had a weakness, and she was determined to find Dugan's.

Whatever it took, she'd find a way to remove Dugan from Rohan's path.

"GET UP ROHAN!" Cormac roared at his young son. Rohan scrambled to get back onto his feet. When he succeeded, his father frowned at him.

"Again!" Cormac ordered.

The bigger boy who had sent Rohan to the ground didn't like

the order. He stood still, a wooden training sword in his hands.

"I am yer laird boy. I told ye, go again." Cormac growled. "Rohan, ye wanted to go riding with Dugan but ye see how little strength ye have."

The older boy offered Rohan a look of pity before he brought his wooden sword into action again. Rohan gritted his teeth, bringing his own wooden sword up to defend himself. There was a solid sound of wood hitting wood. The boys locked, but Rohan's arms just didn't have enough strength to hold the other boy off.

Rohan went rolling through the mud of the training field...again.

This time Cormac lifted Rohan up with a handful of his soiled shirt. Rohan looked at his father, resentment flickering in his eyes.

"Ye think me harsh Rohan, I know it." Cormac said. "But when ye ride out with the retainers, the men ye face will cut ye down if they can. Outside the walls of this stronghold, there is no mercy. Do nae go to the stables again without permission."

"Aye father," Rohan answered.

Blood trickled down his chin from a split lip, but he stood straight and tall. Cormac reached out to ruffle his hair.

"Take heart, Rohan. Ye will grow into a fine man someday."

Cormac pointed his young son back toward the lines of youths training with wooden swords. Rohan retrieved his wooden training sword and went back to his spot. Cormac stood for a moment, watching the way the lads resumed their exercises.

But his attention moved to where Dugan was doing the training. His eldest son was in his prime, his body strong and his motions lethal. He was everything a father might desire in a son and all the things a laird wished for, as well.

Cormac headed back to the warmth of his study, only to find his wife waiting for him.

"You should not have made a mockery of Rohan," Alice growled.

Cormac settled down into his chair. "He tried to go riding

with Dugan."

"Yer bastard knows better than to take him," Alice bit back.

"Aye, Dugan does," Cormac said. "Rohan is the one who needed to be reminded of his place. And so he has been."

"But before all?" Alice wasn't willing to concede the point. "He is yer heir."

"Which is why he must never be allowed to disrespect the order of this stronghold." Cormac flattened his hand on the table in front of him. "Rohan went to the stables where the retainers were, so he was reprimanded in the yard in front of those same men. He will not be coddled."

There was a glint in his wife's eye which warned him that Alice did not agree with him. But she held her tongue and left his study. Her mother's instinct was fierce. He sincerely hoped Rohan had inherited that fire.

One week later

ALICE RETURNED TO the storeroom. It was time to find out what her man had uncovered.

Cray reached up and tugged on his cap once more. "The girl is called Prudence."

Alice wrinkled her nose in response. Cray nodded to assure her she'd heard him correctly.

"Her family is known as Hawlyn, newly arrived from the south. They are fleeing the restoration of the Catholic church that the English queen is demanding of her subjects," Cray continued.

"Protestants?" Alice asked.

"According to those in the market, the family is strictly Puritan," Cray answered.

"Puritans? Are you certain?"

"Aye, Lady," Cray nodded confidently. "There was no missing the way the daughters of the house stood apart from the others in the market. No' a bit of trim on their clothing and they were covered from head to toe. I could not tell ye the color of their hair for how tightly their modesty caps were fitted to their foreheads."

"Sisters?" Alice felt a plan forming.

"There be three girls," Cray explained. "And the soap seller told me there are another three lads, all younger. It seems the master of the house turned to Puritan teachings in the hope of having sons when the third daughter came along."

"Since it appears to have worked, the family has obviously fled all the way to the border in order to maintain their devotion," Alice said, thinking out loud.

"That seems to be so," Cray agreed.

"How old is this girl?" Alice demanded.

Cray frowned. "Well, as I said, she was wrapped up tight."

"Is she a woman or a girl?" Alice clarified.

"Och, well, when they took the…covering garment off her chest, I could see she had a fine pair of…." His mouth rounded in horror when he realized he'd almost said 'tits' in front of his lady.

Alice smiled.

Cray didn't know what to make of her expression.

"Come with me," Alice declared.

PRUDENCE DIDN'T HAVE time to think about Dugan.

The weeks following Samhain were long, filled with days where the family labored hard. The last of the harvest was in but there was still much to do in order to have that food stored properly away for the winter.

Her arms and shoulders ached from how many hours she spent over a large cooking pot. There was not enough room inside, so they'd set up in the yard. Still, she did enjoy the view even if the wind was biting on her nape.

And then there was the thrashing to do.

The barley and wheat needed to be beaten so that the kennels would fall away from the stalks. At first, her brothers found it a fun game, but they tired of it long before the task was finished. And that left Prudence and her sisters in the barn, wielding sticks, their faces covered with fabric to keep the finer particles from filling their noses and making them sneeze. They worked until every last bit of daylight was gone, for the rains would soon begin, making the air moist. They had to get the grain stored away before it became moldy.

There was satisfaction in the work though. Prudence stretched her arms up into the air and heard her neck pop, making her laugh.

"You are due your enjoyment daughter, for you have labored long and hard."

Prudence lowered her arms to find her father watching her. He was a quiet man, who walked on silent steps, and always pondered what he said before opening his mouth.

"Thank you, Father," she answered him.

He'd stopped to inspect one of the large, pottery jugs which was now brimming full of grain.

"This country manor is seen by many as a place of banishment," her father continued. "Yet it provides very well for those of us who are wise enough to see the merit in a simple life."

There were times when Prudence wasn't certain if her father meant his words for her or for himself. She watched the way he scooped up a handful of grain and stared at it.

"The yield was good," she muttered. "We'll have ample bread through Lent."

"Do you see the blessing Daughter?" her father asked earnestly.

Prudence nodded, feeling as though she was missing something. A sense of foreboding was nipping at her.

Her father made a small sound in the back of his throat. "Finish up now. There is supper on the table."

"Yes, fFather."

Prudence picked up a stick to beat her skirts and remove the chaff clinging to her. Her father had departed as quietly as he'd arrived. She saw him making his way toward the house. But when she turned around to cover the opening in the pottery jug with stiff, heavily waxed leather, she gasped.

Laying over the opening of the grain jug was her mask from the Samhain celebration.

Her father had somehow found it.

Well, actually he didn't know for certain what she'd done. But Prudence realized that just making the mask, even if she'd gone no further, would be considered a grave sin by her father. The desire was the true misdeed, for it showed the nature of her soul.

Yet he'd left without a word.

His reasoning dawned upon her as she held the little mask in her hands. A child would be reprimanded and punished, in the hope that they would learn there was a price to pay for disobedience.

An adult, though, was expected to understand that the true accounting of her behavior came at death, when she would face the final judgement.

Her father had decided she was grown.

Well, Samhain bonfires are not for children...

Her cheeks heated as she recalled just how much Dugan had made her feel like a woman.

You have disappointed your father. How can you think of Dugan?

She truly wished it were not so. For she loved her father.

But as she stood there with the mask in her hand, Prudence admitted to herself that what she truly wished was that her father hadn't discovered the mask. She wasn't sorry that she'd gone to the bonfire.

That was the truth inside her heart...

She didn't wish to disappoint her father, but she couldn't devote herself so completely to the time of her death.

Weren't there things to do before then?

The dancing and music had filled her with such a sense of life. Just recalling it made her smile.

No, she wasn't sorry she'd gone.

Prudence walked over to where a small lantern was hanging off a hook. She opened the little tin door and held the mask close to the flame. The fabric caught quickly. She held it up until the flames had licked their way more than halfway through the mask before she dropped it to the ground. She kept a close eye upon it as it burned and turned to ashes, making sure to stomp it several times to ensure no embers survived.

She was grown, which meant she needed to keep from troubling her parents. She knew their beliefs well. If she chose to act differently, then it was her job to keep such news from them, lest she distress them.

Of course, her father would not appreciate her thoughts. But she couldn't lie to herself and claim to agree with her parents completely.

Was that sinful?

Perhaps.

But at least there was comfort in knowing that she alone would answer for her actions.

CHAPTER FIVE

Hay land

"MY LADY?" ORAN tilted his head, a perplexed look upon his face. Clearly the veteran retainer hadn't expected his mistress waiting for him in the stables.

"I spoke clearly enough," Alice said, aiming a withering look at the retainer. "You should understand my instructions."

Unlike Cray, Oran was no lad, but a mature, seasoned man. Several scars decorated his forearms lending testimony to his experience in battle.

"Perhaps it might be best to wait for the laird to return," Oran stated quietly. "He's only gone up to Lindsey land."

"If my husband were here..." She stressed the word 'husband', "I would take the matter straight to him. However, winter's breath is already blowing on the back of our necks. I shall not leave that girl at the mercy of Puritan parents should she find herself with child."

"The way Cray tells it, they were no' together long enough for such a thing to happen," Oran insisted.

"Men often think in such a way," Alice added. "Yet it is a woman who will be cast out in her shift if she is considered soiled. I understand this girl is from a Puritan family. Just the knowledge that she was with Dugan, a Scot, is enough to have her considered ruined. It will bring a curse on us all...even a failed harvest perhaps. It is my duty as mistress of this castle to see her provided for."

Oran was wavering. A failed harvest was a horrific thing, the sort of catastrophe which had to be avoided at any cost. Even doubt had to give way to making certain bad luck didn't fall on the fields of the next season. Alice knew it was the perfect threat.

"Aye ma'am," Oran replied in a tired voice. "And if she will nae come with me?"

"Ye are not a young man, Oran," Alice informed him sternly. "You know what you have to do. It has likely never occurred to her that the family she breaks bread with might cast her into the gutter. She is young and likely to make a foolish choice. You mustn't blame her though—leaving one's family is difficult. I expect ye to bring her along for all our sakes, including hers."

Oran reached up and tugged on his cap.

Alice didn't linger in the stable. She wasn't going to give the man the chance to argue the matter further. She needed Oran and his men away before her husband returned.

Cormac Hay wouldn't fail to see what she was about. Alice knew it. Yet there would be little the laird could do if the girl was already on Hay land. He wouldn't be able to send her back, not to a Puritan family. Her reputation would be beyond repair.

And then there was Dugan. As devoted as her husband's bastard was to his honor, he'd wed the girl without delay.

Which was precisely what Alice wanted to happen.

This time, Dugan wouldn't be able to gain back the favor of the Hay retainers—not if he was wed to an Englishwoman. Scots might forgive being born a bastard, but they would never forget the blemish of wedding on the wrong side of the border.

Cormac would be furious with her, of course.

Yet the deed would be accomplished. Alice didn't need Cormac to like her. She'd born his son, so her position was secure.

All she had to do was ensure that Dugan was kept too busy to ride after Oran.

Erin appeared almost in the same moment that Alice took up her place in the large chair at the end of the great hall. Next to the hearth, it was a place of honor.

"Mistress? Did you wish me to fetch something for you?"

"Fetch Dugan to me."

Erin was obviously curious as to why. Still, as the mistress of the house, Alice didn't have to explain herself to a maid. Even if the girl was Cormac's spy, she was still a servant.

And while Cormac was away on Lindsey land, Dugan was bound to answer to Alice as well. At long last, she was free to do what was necessary to ensure Dugan would not stand in Rohan's path to the lairdship.

England

"FATHER FOUND MY mask."

Modesty stiffened. She had her apron pulled up in one hand as she searched out eggs in the hens' nesting holes. After looking around to make sure they were alone, she locked gazes with Prudence.

"What did he say?"

"Naught," Prudence replied.

Modesty's eyes narrowed.

"You should burn yours," Prudence said softly. "I should have done so the moment we were back." Hindsight wouldn't help her, but it might well save her sister.

Modesty nodded.

"What are you going to do?" Modesty asked.

"I do not believe there is anything to be done," Prudence answered. "He left the mask without a word, and in doing so, I believe he was making it clear that he was washing his hands of the matter."

Modesty was silent for a long moment.

"I admit, I would almost be glad of a reprimand," Prudence admitted. "For now, it seems I have been separated from his guidance."

There was noise from the yard. Modesty and Prudence went around the stone wall which had the hen holes built inside of it and saw four horses in front of the house. They snorted, their breath white in the air. The men riding them dismounted as their oldest brother came down to take the horses toward the stable along with one of their visitors.

"Guests?" Modesty muttered. "I am surprised."

So was Prudence. A chill touched her nape as she and her sister headed back up to the house. They entered through the kitchen, stopping to carefully place the new eggs in a bowl.

Their mother came in, her pace hurried.

"Modesty…there you are…" She came around the worktable and looked intently at Modesty. "Wash your face and hands. Our guests wish to see you."

"Yes mother," Modesty muttered before she went over to where the copper pot still had hot water in it, gently steaming. She ladled up some into the wash bowl before adding cold water from a pitcher. She turned to look at her mother. "They wish to look at me?" Modesty asked.

Their mother nodded. "You are at an age for a match to be arranged."

Modesty looked at Prudence with wide eyes.

"Prudence, you are to do the washing by yourself today," their mother instructed.

Her mother knew about the mask…

There was a clipped, cold edge to her words. If Prudence had had any doubt about what her father knew, that doubt was dispelled as she looked at her mother to find a harsh look of disapproval on her face.

"Mother," Modesty implored. "You have always sent us to do laundry together, lest one of us slip into the river."

"That is true," their mother said. "For family is a blessing. Yet it is earned through obedience to the commandments."

Honor thy mother and father….

This was her father's way of reprimanding her—denying her the comfort of another member of the family while she toiled.

Prudence turned toward the doorway to save her sister from incriminating herself. With eight people in the house, there was always washing to do. Any day without rain would see the laundry taking priority over inside chores.

"Be…careful, Prudence."

Prudence glanced back to see her mother watching her and worrying the fabric of her skirt. But she appeared to be resolved in sending Prudence out to the river alone.

"Yes, Mother."

She moved toward the back door where a basket of soiled undergarments waited for her. Prudence hefted it up and headed for the river.

Many people drowned while doing laundry…

She'd have to take care, especially since she was alone. The water was so cold that when one was first submerged, one would gasp uncontrollably. As well, the sturdy English wool her dress was made of was a good thing when dry, but if she went into the river, those same water-laden wool skirts would become very heavy, further dragging her down.

In many places, there were tiny docks built for women to kneel upon when they were scrubbing and rinsing garments.

Not so here.

Prudence looked at the flowing water of the river, trying to choose the safest place. There was little point in scrubbing near the shallows, for all she'd do was stir up mud. Dead leaves were thick along the banks as well, so in order to wash the laundry correctly, she'd need to venture further out into the current.

Complaining will serve you not…

At least she might indulge in her mental fascination about Dugan, for there was no one to see her.

And just those thoughts of the Scot would keep her warm.

Scotland

IT WAS STARTING to snow.

It wouldn't stick yet. But that didn't change how cold the tip of Dugan's nose was. He tugged his bonnet further down to keep his ears warm but the knitted cap was already at his eyebrows. Brody grunted beside him.

"I cannae believe we've been sent on this fool's errand." Brody made a sound in the back of his throat. "What could lady Hay think to gain by sending us after her husband? Lindsey land borders our own, the man will nae get lost."

Dugan was surprised as well.

And suspicious.

Yet by the time the Lindsey stronghold came into sight, Dugan was too cold and hungry to care much about what lady Alice was about.

The Lindsey retainers allowed him in through the main gate. One of the Lindsey captains stood in the yard as Dugan and Brody dismounted. Dugan gave his horse an affectionate pat before one of the Lindseys led it away toward the stables.

"Ye're Laird Hay's bastard," the captain stated.

"I am," Dugan replied. That description was something he'd grown accustomed to.

"Come along," the captain said. "Yer father is in the hall with my laird."

Dugan reached up and tugged on the corner of his cap, then the captain turned and led the way. Inside the main keep, there was a double wide opening which led to the great hall. Several tables were there, close to the large hearth. Dugan agreed that it was chilly but the fire blazing in the hearth suggested that there was a blizzard raging outside.

As he moved closer to where his father sat, Dugan realized why the Lindsey staff had built up the fire.

Laird Lindsey was a frail man.

His hair was white and tufts of it poked out from beneath his knitted bonnet. The chair he sat in had a thick highland cowhide draped over it so that the fur might help protect the man from drafts. He was in good humor though, laughing with Dugan's father.

The captain walked closer, and both lairds looked up to see Dugan.

Laird Hay gestured Dugan forward. "Dugan, me boy, come closer."

Dugan tugged on the corner of his cap as he stopped in front of his sire.

"This is Dugan," Laird Hay said, introducing him. "Me bastard."

Laird Lindsey contemplated Dugan for a long moment.

"A grown son is a good thing to have," Laird Lindsey declared.

"No if ye ask me lady wife!" Laird Hay declared with a chuckle.

Laird Lindsey lifted his hand and waved it across the air. "She wants her own son to follow ye. Which is natural enough. But he's barely off the breast."

Dugan watched his father. Laird Hay knew well the art of being in charge of a clan. Every matter was weighed before commented upon.

"I see what ye are thinking," Laird Lindsey continued. "Yer lady wife is from fine lineage. Such a thing matters in this world, but none of us choose when the boat man comes for us, heh? I wager ye sleep better at night knowing ye have Dugan here, should ye end yer days before yer legitimate son is a man."

Dugan knew the set to his sire's eyes. Laird Hay didn't care for the conversation. "Why are ye here Dugan?" his father asked, turning toward him.

Dugan tugged on his cap once more. Aye, he was being overly attentive to his manners, but it was better than being accused of forgetting his place.

And there were a lot of eyes upon him at that moment.

"Lady Hay worries that ye do nae see the signs of winter," Dugan offered.

Laird Lindsey let out a bark of laughter, then slapped his thigh before he pointed at Laird Hay. "By the way yer lady wife orders ye home, I'd think she'd have more than two babes to show for her attention to ye!"

The Lindseys were amused by their laird's words. The hall filled with their laughter. But Laird Hay merely smiled.

The expression was forced. Dugan knew it.

And Laird Lindsey didn't miss it, either.

"Here now man." Laird Lindsey sobered. "Do nae deny me my amusements. If we can nae laugh at one another's wives, we're hardly fit to call ourselves lairds!"

This time, Laird Hay chuckled. He lifted his mug in a toast.

"Lad," Laird Lindsey said, looking at Dugan. "There is good in being whelped on the wrong side of the blanket, for ye will nae have to suffer someone bringing ye home a lady to wed!"

The hall filled with laughter again. Dugan couldn't help smiling.

"Would that I might be bastard born as well!" A newcomer raised his voice above the chuckling.

"Ha!" Laird Lindsey declared as he pointed at the man arriving. "Ye're me spawn and I cannae deny it, for ye are every bit as much a compatriot of Lucifer as I ever was! If I was nae there when ye were born, I'd doubt yer mother was yer dam. Ye have not a single bit of her calm demeanor in ye, Ruben."

Ruben stopped next to Dugan and tugged on his cap in deference to the two lairds at the table.

"I suppose I should send ye off in the morning," Laird Lindsey remarked as he sobered. "Ruben, take Dugan here off somewhere. I need to settle yer sister's future with Laird Hay's son. The boat man is coming for me, I ken it."

"Father—" Ruben protested.

But Laird Lindsey made a slashing motion with his hand. "Do nae argue with me like a woman. Anyone with eyes can see my bones sticking out of me skin. I am wasting away. Time to complete a father's matters concerning his eldest daughter. For all me jesting about the burden of lady wives, mine was correct to send Laird Hay a letter. A laird should make sure his children are settled before he heads on to see St. Peter. Off with ye both. This is the business of old men."

Ruben reached for his bonnet again, accepting his father's will.

Dugan mimicked the gesture, then they both left. Behind them, Laird Lindsey began to speak in a low tone as the business of the clan was conducted.

"I was nae jesting," Ruben confided to Dugan once they were well away from the great hall. "Me father has been intent on securing matches for us all."

"Ye have no desire to wed?" Dugan asked bluntly.

Ruben shrugged. "It is nae that. But the Douglases have decided I should have one of their daughters."

"The Douglases are powerful," Dugan offered.

"The lass is eleven winters old, man," Ruben exclaimed. "If I say I find her agreeable, I expect ye to smash me in the jaw, for it's indecent, no matter what we might be to one another in the future."

"Well, it looks as if ye will nae be settling down anytime soon," Dugan remarked with a grin. "I will do me best to help ye pass the time."

Ruben's lips twitched and parted into a grin. "Spring can nae arrive soon enough!"

England

"MODESTY…" TEMPERANCE WHISPERED after their lantern had

been extinguished for the night. "Do you want to wed him?"

Modesty blew out a frustrated breath that was loud in the dark room. "How should I know? Father introduced me and sent me straight on to the kitchen to prove my housewife skills by cooking a meal."

"But I heard that father agreed to a match between you both," Temperance added.

"I know that well enough," Modesty exclaimed. "Yet I truly cannot tell you what color his eyes are, for he never looked at me."

Temperance was quiet, but not for long. The sounds of her whimpers filled the room.

"Honestly Temperance, I am the one being wed to a stranger," Modesty declared. "Why are you weeping?"

"Because I shall be next..." Temperance hiccupped. "After Prudence, of course."

"All the more reason to save your tears until a moment arrives which tests you beyond your control," Prudence advised her younger sister. "Without a doubt, it will come."

"Well spoken," Modesty agreed.

Now if Prudence could only manage to heed her own advice. Her eyes were stinging with unshed tears. She drew in a deep breath, attempting to dispel them, for they were born of pity.

The midnight well wouldn't have its way when it came to her fate. Temperance was correct. Matches would be made for all of them in turn. There was an order to life, one which yielded confidence in the future, at least for her parents.

And she'd taste that apple and see Dugan's face in her dreams until the day she died.

It was simply the way real life was.

Longing was like a flame flickering inside of her. It was far too late to lament her choices, which had led to her meeting Dugan. But she wouldn't wish to forget him either. Not when he'd shown her that she might feel so intensely alive.

The door moved.

Was their father checking to make certain they were all in bed?

It appeared so, for the door opened and the doorway was filled with a large frame. Only the person didn't linger, but came straight inside the little room in a flash.

He was followed by others.

Prudence gasped. She might have screamed but whoever was in the room didn't give her the chance. She barely finished her swift intake of breath before a hand covered her mouth. She kicked but another man was kneeling on the bedding, holding her captive.

"Not a sound out of ye…or I shall cut down whoever comes to yer aid."

Scots?

Prudence felt her eyes bulging wide in horror.

Scots had often raided the English.

And they did… Well, she didn't know the details of what they did, only that it was horrible and to be feared.

There was a spark as a flint was struck. It fell into a little pewter bowl which was full of chaff. The dry husks caught easily, a bright yellow flame licking its way upward. The Scot held the candle from their lantern over it and the wick caught.

In the darkness, the single flame was bright, casting a circle of light over their modest beds and the men who had invaded their maiden's chamber.

"Which one of you is Prudence?"

The candle illuminated the face of the Scot who asked the question.

It wasn't Dugan.

Prudence felt her heart constrict as she looked at him. Fear nipped at her, but she realized it wasn't for herself.

When he spoke her name, she froze, no longer trying to pry the fingers off her mouth. She'd brought danger to her sisters. The guilt which descended onto her shoulders was crushing.

"Come now," the Scot continued. "Tell me who is Prudence

and I will leave the other two be. No need for yer mother to lose all three of her daughters at once."

Lose...

Now she was afraid for herself.

But Prudence still worried more about her sisters. Temperance was but fifteen. Too young to die.

You are only nineteen...

She was and it appeared she would have to be content with her meager number of years. Prudence lifted her hand up, but Modesty snorted, and did the same.

Thankfully, Temperance was too terrified to move.

"Cray," the Scot called. "Get in here and tell me which of the two is the one Dugan met."

They were Dugan's kin at least.

That should not give you comfort!

After all, she had no idea what sort of man Dugan was. And even if she had trusted in their brief encounter, his kin could be an altogether different matter.

They were Scots, after all.

The leader shifted to the side, clearing the doorway and allowing the light to illuminate the men outside who had their swords drawn.

The single candlelight bathed those long lengths of steel, showing off the sharpened edges and the confident way they were gripped.

Prudence's parents' disapproval was suddenly naught compared to the idea of them being cut down because of her mistake.

Prudence pointed at herself.

The Scot peered at her intently, moving the candle so that it shone in her face. A younger man came through the doorway— Prudence recognized him as one of the men who had stood around Dugan.

"Is this the one, Cray?"

Modesty tried to speak, but her words were muffled.

"They are both claiming to be the one we're after," the first

Scot said in a frustrated voice. "I don't care to deal with two females who will need minding all the way home. If ye're able to recall which is the correct one, we can take the one Lady Hay has sent us for."

Cray looked at Prudence and then over at Modesty. He scratched his head while he pondered the question.

"The one we seek is shorter than her sister," Cray suddenly recalled. He smiled at his superior. "We are looking for the shorter one."

Prudence was on her feet before her next breath.

Relief washed through her as Modesty was placed next to her.

The Scot in front of them narrowed his eyes.

"Not a peep…or I'll run yer kin through," he warned them again.

His voice was hard, much like the hands holding Prudence in place next to her sister. What was worse was the thought of her little brothers lying dead in the yard.

"I am Prudence."

But it was Modesty who spoke.

"She is not," Prudence argued. "I am known as Prudence."

"That's the one!" Cray exclaimed as he pointed at her. "I recall the voice."

"This one is slouching," the man behind Modesty stated. He gripped her by the neck. "It's a noble trait to want to protect yer sister, but Cray knows who we seek. Straighten up now. Better one, than both of ye gone, ye ken? Think of yer mother, lass."

Modesty didn't have much of a choice. The man squeezed her neck, and she lifted her shoulders to try and save herself from the pain. He released her, leaving her standing at her full height, before she gasped, and hunched over again.

"Too late for that ploy, mistress," the leader remarked. "Gag and bind her well."

Fear tore through Prudence.

But it was for her sisters.

The hand over her mouth lifted away for a moment as another man came forward with a length of knotted linen he intended to push into her mouth.

Prudence fell to her knees. "Do not harm my sisters. I beg you."

The men trying to bind her hadn't expected her to kneel. They dove after her, grabbing for her hands.

She wanted to resist—every fiber of her body seemed to be screaming for her to fight. Prudence quelled the demands. Better that she suffer her fate alone.

"Ye come along quiet, and I will not hurt yer siblings," the man stated.

Prudence heard the doubt in his tone—he didn't really trust her—and so she wasn't surprised when his men tied her wrists together and gagged her.

And she suffered through it without protest.

It was only as she was being lifted up and onto the back of a horse did she remember that she had brought this upon herself.

She only had herself to blame.

CHAPTER SIX

Her abductors didn't rest until they were on the other side of the border.

Prudence had never spent so many hours on a horse. Her thighs were numb, and her lower back hurt more than it ever had. Yet it was the chill that tormented her the most.

At least you have a long dress on...

Her family's new Puritan ways included sleeping in a long, loose gown which went over her shift. The garment had a collar, like a shirt, and she was extremely grateful for it as the hours of the night passed and they rode on. Heading north meant the temperature wasn't going to get any warmer. When at last the leader of the group called for them to stop, Prudence slid off the horse she rode and crumpled.

She growled and struggled to stand.

No matter how much her pride would have liked for her body to obey, she was only halfway to her feet when the leader pulled her the rest of the way up with a firm grip on her bicep.

"Stomp yer feet lass," he advised her.

She did as he said, desperate for relief from needing to be held up. Her legs hurt as the circulation resumed. Her knees wobbled but at least they held.

Small mercies...

Suddenly, the leader pressed his dirk against her wrist, and she gasped in horror. Her eyes widened as she looked at the sun shining on the polished surface of the blade.

"I certainly did nae bring ye all this way just to kill ye lass," he muttered as he jerked the blade up and slit the strip of cloth which had bound her wrists together. "Go on and see to yer needs," he said, jerking his head toward several trees. The sound of water hitting stones made her cheeks burn with a blush as she realized the men riding with them had simply lifted their kilts to relieve themselves.

Prudence scurried around the tree, grateful for how thick the trunks were. Now that she was off the horse, she did need to relieve herself.

Immediately…

The moment she found relief, she tore the gag off. Normally she would have abhorred waste, but she threw it to the ground with satisfaction, uncaring that the strip of cloth might have been put to good use in mending garments.

"Come back here, Mistress."

She could run.

And how far do you think you will get?

Once again, her pride didn't care very much for the answer. At least she was unbound.

And you can't go home, or he'll just follow you and do what he threatened to do…

No, she absolutely could not go home, or else her family would suffer. There truly were fates worse than death. Living with the knowledge that she'd caused the deaths of her family was something she simply could not suffer.

Prudence squared her shoulders. The choice was clear, and she refused to be a coward about it. The first step was the hardest, but she took it, and then the next one. She made it back around the clump of trees and saw her abductor watching for her. The stern expression on his face eased a bit when she came into view. There might even have been a hint of respect in his eyes as she closed the distance.

"Here—" The leader thrust his hand out toward her.

In his hand was a bundle of her clothing. Her skirt was

wrapped up around the rest of it. A happy little smile lifted her lips. She reached out and hugged it close, grateful beyond measure. Just yesterday, she'd thought she had nothing. But today, she realized how rich she'd been to have her family and the simple dignity of clothing.

"Aye, I thought ye'd be glad of having something to put on."

How could she smile at him?

Prudence chastised herself as she went back around the cluster of trees and unrolled the bundle. A prisoner or not, she was grateful for her clothing. Even her shoes were nestled inside the fabric of her skirt. She happily removed her long robe and pulled her stockings on, making sure to secure the top of each on with a leather garter before slipping her feet into her shoes.

Simple necessities…

She was beyond grateful as she worked to dress herself. There was something about being dressed which bolstered her confidence. The sturdy wool cut the morning chill and her shoes were a welcome relief from bare feet. Even her linen cap was there, thanks to her mother's insistence that everything be kept neat and orderly. Pulling it over her hair restored her peace of mind as well.

As if your clothing will stop them from doing whatever they please with you…

She knew that was the truth. Still, feelings didn't often make logical sense, now did they? Besides, there was nothing to gain by being angry. Prudence ordered her emotions to settle down before she returned to the other side of the tree. If her only choice was dignity or none, well, she'd maintain her composure. Pride might be considered poor comfort, but the gag had been very dry, and she'd rather not suffer it again.

When she stood in front of the leader once more, he studied her for a long moment. It almost appeared as though he was as ill at ease with their circumstances as she was.

"I am Oran," the leader said, introducing himself.

Manners were something her mother had trained her in since

before Prudence could recall. She started to lower herself into a reverence, then stopped, and hovered for a moment halfway down.

Oran made a little 'huraph' sound.

"I suppose this is not the sort of introduction where the manners yer mother taught ye apply," Oran remarked wryly.

Prudence straightened up.

"Here." Oran thrust a flask toward her. "Drink and eat, for I swear I'll tie ye over the saddle like a sack of grain if ye faint. We've no time to be coddling ye. Winter is closing its grip on us."

The horse snorted, and she quickly lifted the flask to her lips. It was a good thing she was famished because the oat cakes smelled strongly of the leather bag they had been stored in. Yet there was also a faint aroma of nutty oats. Her belly rumbled, demanding substance.

Consuming her meager meal took very little time. She didn't lose a single crumb. Yet all too soon Oran was whistling, calling his men to order. He appeared to be checking his horse's bridle, but she knew he was waiting to see if she'd comply with his summons.

What choice did she have?

England

THE HAWLYN HOUSE was silent.

It was so quiet, Modesty could clearly hear the boiling of the water in the copper. Nobody moved. The household staff remained idle instead of attending to the ever-needed work in the kitchen. The master of the house stood with his back to his family, facing the hearth.

Even young James, at only six winters, had his ankles crossed beneath the table instead of swinging his feet back and forth in his usual way.

There was a stiff intake of breath from her father, then he finally turned to face his family.

"We must be grateful for the lack of spilled blood," he muttered solemnly.

Modesty's mother sniffled. For a moment, she and her husband locked gazes.

"Prudence did not keep her feet on the path of obedience," her father stated firmly. "She should be thankful her actions did not bring harm to her sisters or family."

"Father, you cannot mean to say you believe Prudence deserved to be…abducted," Modesty declared.

Her father turned to her. "Your sister," he said, "chose wildness and sinful celebrations. I have made great efforts to teach her the dangers of such endeavors, yet she chose not to heed the lesson."

"I told you both not to go to the bonfire," Temperance grumbled.

Her eyes widened when she realized what she'd said. She bit her lower lip, but it was far too late.

"You went as well, Modesty?"

Modesty's father's tone was hard. Disapproval shimmered in his eyes as he waited for her to answer. The room was silent as a tomb while all eyes rested on her.

"I did," Modesty admitted.

Her father shifted his gaze to his youngest daughter.

"And you knew of this, Temperance?"

Temperance's eyes filled with tears which streamed down her cheeks under her father's direct gaze. She looked toward her mother but found no comfort in her eyes. Temperance nodded and hung her head in shame. Her tears fell onto the worn wood surface of the table.

Master Hawlyn snorted. "This is the fruit of disobedience!"

James looked at his father with disbelief. "Father, you never raise your voice. You say it shows a lack of self-discipline."

His young voice appeared to temper his father's anger. Master Hawlyn snapped his mouth shut while he wrestled with his anger.

"Thank you for reminding me, James," Master Hawlyn said to his youngest son before he directed his attention toward his daughters. "Innocence…is priceless, and unmatched in this world. It is also fragile. Once it has been tarnished, there is no cleaning away the stain."

He drew in another deep breath and locked his hands behind his back but the look he sent Modesty was hard and unrelenting.

"Your sister's plight must serve as an example to you, Modesty. Henceforth, you will sleep in the eves. I suggest you devote yourself to prayer, and try to amend your willful nature, before you meet with the same fate your sister has."

⇸⟩⟩⟩✕⟨⟨⟨⇷

"MODESTY?" TEMPERANCE CALLED out in a ghost of a whisper after the lamp was extinguished.

The bed they had was small enough that she really didn't need to speak any louder. The section of the eves they were afforded to sleep in was tiny too, and the roof was directly above them, so it was cold and sleeping together was very practical.

"Do you believe Prudence deserves to be…wherever she is?" Temperance continued, in spite of a lack of response from her sister.

"There is little point in talking about the matter," Modesty answered.

"Are you angry with me?" Temperance asked. "I truly did not intend to tell father about the bonfire. I was simply so worried about Prudence."

Modesty sighed. "I am worried about her as well."

"What shall we do?"

"We must hope fate is kind to her," Modesty replied.

Modesty tried to use a hopeful tone, but the truth was, she

didn't have much faith in her sister meeting with a kind end. Scots were uncivilized at best, savages at worst. They had no love for the English, no matter how little choice anyone had in just where they were born.

Yet there had a been a moment at that bonfire when it hadn't mattered what side of the border any of them had been born on. Scot and English, Protestant, Catholic and Puritan had mingled and laughed together freely. They had been just people, celebrating the joy of a bountiful harvest. It was a tradition older than any of their disagreements.

Perhaps the Laird of Misrule had sent for his queen consort. Perhaps the Midnight Well was more enchanted than anyone knew. Modesty would like to think her sister was bound for love instead of ruin…or the very practical arranged match she would likely have to endure.

Guilt gnawed at Modesty for thinking of her own plight when her sister was in such dire circumstances. But even as she admitted her guilt, she recalled the way the Laird of Misrule had protected her sister at the bonfire. He was a man of principle.

Modesty allowed the memory to linger in her mind while she fell asleep. For doing so afforded her hope. No matter how much her logic wanted to argue against it—what were the chances that the Lord of Misrule was behind Prudence's abduction?—hope always did manage to maintain its flame against the darkness of disappearance.

The last thing to cross her mind was a prayer that her sister would find some hope in her circumstances.

Or at least a quick death.

CHAPTER SEVEN

"WELL, YE'RE NOT very much to look at, are ye?"

Lady Hay was peering at Prudence, her lips pressed in disapproval. "No manners either."

Oran was a single pace behind her after marching her up the main aisle of the great hall. He flattened his hand on her shoulder, pushing her down until Prudence reverenced.

The respectful gesture didn't gain her any kind looks from those watching.

Members of the Hay clan had started to gather around now. Maids, other household staff, and retainers were there as well, their harder frames making it nearly impossible for Prudence to calm her racing heart.

Were they planning to kill her?

Lady Hay shook her head and made a motion with her hand for Prudence to rise. Oran cupped her elbow and made sure she was quick to obey his lady's commands. Prudence popped back up and had to widen her stance to avoid stumbling forward.

There was a round of judgmental chuckles at her expense.

"I see no cause for amusement." Lady Hay snapped.

The people around Prudence quieted down, but there was more than one disgruntled look sent her way. Prudence might have been concerned about that, but the truth was, she was almost too exhausted to care. She hadn't slept in the past two days.

Lady Hay leaned forward in her chair. "I had to send good

Hay men down to the borderlands to fetch you here."

"Why?" Prudence asked.

Lady Hay was a very pretty woman. But she'd heard that being shrewish destroyed even the most beautiful of faces, and when the lady sent her a scathing look, Prudence realized it was the truth.

"Who are ye to speak without permission?" Lady Hay demanded.

"I would like to know why she is here as well." A voice boomed from the other end of the hall. A man stood there, shrugging out of his surcoat. Clumps of snow dripped onto the floor as everyone instantly shifted and lowered themselves.

Even lady Hay rose from the large chair she'd been sitting so regally in.

"My laird husband," the lady muttered very sweetly. Prudence couldn't help staring at the meek way the lady had sunk into a curtsey, holding it as her husband came down the aisle with heavy footfalls.

He stopped in front of Prudence. Oran pushed on her shoulder again. This time, Prudence offered the reverence with more sincerity.

"Do nae be making the lass bob up and down, Oran." Laird Hay gave her a quick gesture to rise. "She has not a clue who I am, and she appears to be ready to drop from fatigue. Ye must have ridden straight through."

"We did." Oran reached up and tugged on the corner of his cap, earning a grunt from his laird.

Prudence straightened up, and Laird Hay looked her over from head to toe.

"Who are ye lass?" he asked.

"Prudence Hawlyn sir," she answered.

His eyebrows rose before he turned to glare at Lady Hay. The lady rose but remained silent. There was no hint of remorse in her attitude. Laird Hay stomped up the three steps to the high ground where the chairs were sitting. He turned and sat down with a swish of his kilt.

"My dear lady wife," the laird said. "What could have possessed ye to have an English girl brought into this stronghold?"

"I believe I am the cause."

Prudence remembered Dugan's voice.

It was as if she'd only parted from him, with only a few moments passed, instead of nearly two weeks, for her body responded instantly.

And intensely.

Her heart skipped.

And then beat twice as fast.

Prudence turned her head and lifted her chin to meet his eyes. Somehow, the darkness of that evening had masked just how fearsome Dugan was. Perhaps she'd been enchanted, as her father had warned her could happen at such pagan gatherings. Because now she discovered herself trembling and she stepped back from the imposing Highlander in front of her. This was not a man to trifle with.

And he was very displeased by the sight of her.

"Ye know this lass, Dugan?" Laird Hay asked.

Dugan looked toward the high ground. He reached up and tugged on his cap, making it clear that the man seated on that dais was in fact the laird of the clan and master of the house.

His word would be law...

And the burly retainers surrounding her would see it enforced.

"I should say he knows her," Lady Hay answered for Dugan. "She is his consort."

There was a gasp from the women watching. Conversation rippled through the assembled crowd.

Laird Hay turned his head to look at his wife. "The lass is covered from head to toe. I can nae even see a single strand of her hair. She does nae look the sort to be a lightskirt."

Prudence felt her cheeks heat. "I certainly am not."

"And yet," Lady Hay glared at her. "I hear Dugan danced

around a bonfire with you, after accepting you as his consort."

After she finished speaking, Lady Hay sat down next to her husband. Her position was a proclamation of her power within the Hay household. Only those women of very high birth were allowed to be by their husbands' side during official business.

Prudence felt her heartrate accelerate again.

Her breathing was rapid too and Dugan must have heard it, for he shifted his eyes toward her for a moment.

Why did her composure desert her?

If she was to meet a horrible fate, could she at least do so with her dignity intact? A tickle of sweat ran down the side of her face, confirming that she was to be denied even that small request. Everyone likely saw her shaking. For the first time in her life, she truly wished she knew a word of profanity.

"Dugan..." Laird Hay sounded exasperated as he made a motion with his hand for Dugan to start explaining.

"I did go to a Samhain bonfire," Dugan stated clearly.

"He boldly became the Laird of Misrule," Lady Hay added. "And bolder still, he did so on the English side of the border."

There was another outbreak of amusement from those watching, but this laughter was more encouragement than disapproval.

Lady Hay slapped the armrest of her chair in agitation. "When one is the son of the laird, he must consider the consequences of every action," Lady Hay insisted.

"As to that bit," Laird Hay said, "ye are me son and must be aware of the weight of the clan honor on yer shoulders."

For the first time, Lady Hay seemed to lose some of her confidence. The laird had stressed the word 'son' which appeared to displease his lady wife.

"Dugan must understand the ramifications of his misadventures," Lady Hay declared.

"I committed no transgression," Dugan protested, seeming to be losing his patience. "I do nae care to see this lass brought here."

"Isn't it just like a man to think naught of the reputation of a lass he dallies with. Yer own state of illegitimacy is the result of a lack of respect for what happens to a woman when she makes a poor choice regarding her virtue."

Dugan's lips pressed into a hard line, visibly wrestling with his temper. He turned back to look toward the dais, clearly waiting for the laird to decide the matter.

"Celebrating Samhain with a bit of dancing is no cause for such actions, wife," Laird Hay growled.

"This girl is from a Puritan family," Lady Hay informed her husband.

Prudence found herself the subject of scrutiny once more. But Laird Hay looked back at his wife. "Make yer point, Alice. The Hay do nae steal daughters. What ye have done can nae be undone. Dugan is not the only one who needs to be reminded of the weight of the clan honor on their shoulders."

There was a rumble of approval from the crowd.

"What I have done," Alice said, "is keep every Hay soul safe from the wages of sin." She pointed at Prudence. "Dugan left this girl to the unkindness of fate after trifling with her. A stain such as that can never be washed away. Not in the eyes of her Puritan family."

Lady Hay knew how to choose her words.

You mean twist them...

Prudence decided her inner voice was correct, for the lady hadn't really said anything untrue. Yet the way her words were strung together made them damning, even without substance.

Prudence felt as if she had her foot caught in a snare. The need to struggle was nearly overwhelming.

"A bit of Samhain dancing is hardly reason to send Hay re-tainers across the border," Laird Hay snarled.

"I sent Oran to fetch her because if her family learns of the matter, she will likely be put out," Alice insisted. "Puritans do not even have convents for daughters who stray from the path of obedience. Shall we wager our good fortune against the uncertainty of this sordid secret being learned? How can we expect blessings in the spring if one of the laird's own family is responsible for a girl being tossed out into the cruel jaws of winter? Her ghost will haunt our fields."

There was a stiffening among those watching. Expressions grew serious, proving that the lady knew her people well.

And just how to multiply their fears.

Dugan turned to look at her. His gaze was so piercing, it felt as though he was looking straight into her soul. Panic was gripping her and yet Prudence felt the need to stand up for herself. She was not a weakling.

"I did not ask anything of him," Prudence said, looking toward the lady and laird. "It was but a Samhain bonfire."

"A Hay retainer must understand his responsibilities while wearing the colors of this clan," Alice informed her decisively. "Even masked, his colors would be noted."

So everyone knew who she'd been dancing with. A stain on one's honor could never be cleaned away. Prudence heard her father's words ringing in her ears. Around her, she saw eyes narrow, condemning her for her lack of self-discipline. Prudence straightened her shoulders.

"The guilt of not seeking permission from my family is mine, lady," Prudence answered clearly. "As such, I must shoulder the responsibility."

"And yet, this is now a matter which involves a member of my family because Dugan was wearing Hay colors," Alice continued. "Life is difficult enough without having a black mark against us in the eyes of the saints and the Lord. If yer family had cast you out, Dugan's actions would have been judged by all who are holy."

There was another round of rumbling in the hall. Prudence felt the weight of judgement as the members of the Hay clan cast their gazes toward her. It wasn't really about who believed what the lady was saying.

No, the true matter was the fact that no one was willing to

take the chance that fate would agree with Alice Hay. Luck, and the favor of the saints? That did matter. Several of the people around her were making the sign of the cross over themselves or touching their small saints' medals.

"What precisely are ye suggesting we do about this?" Laird Hay asked his wife, clearly displeased with her but wise enough to notice how many of his people were being swayed by her argument.

"It is simple enough." Alice smiled. "They should be married immediately."

The laird's face turned red. He glared at his wife and gripped the armrests of his chair. His fingers were curled into talons with his fury.

"Remove this girl from me sight."

JUST AS PRUDENCE had expected, the laird's word was law.

At the same time that the laird's order rang through the hall, she felt hands on her, gripping and pulling on her arms. She stumbled because she was trying to turn around and whoever had hold of her arm didn't give her a chance to do so.

She just managed to keep herself from falling.

"Clumsy. I cannot imagine why Dugan decided to dance with ye."

"You might afford me the chance to turn around," Prudence declared.

The woman who had hold of Prudence scoffed at her. "You might recognize that it's best to get gone when the laird is so displeased with ye!"

"Leaving suits me very well," Prudence said.

The woman hadn't been expecting Prudence to agree with her. She contemplated Prudence through narrowed eyes before she released her.

"Don't fall behind. I've things to do other than deal with ye," the woman said.

She offered Prudence another huff before turning and starting to make her way through the kitchens. The scent of roasting meat and fresh bread made Prudence's mouth water. But the woman didn't stop.

Prudence's belly rumbled, confirming the oat cakes were long gone. There were several long worktables laden with fare. Servants were arranging plates, clearly making ready to serve a meal now that their laird had returned.

The woman headed away from the food and the hall where it would be served. With every step, the hearths were left further behind, which meant the air grew cooler.

Was the woman going to throw her out into the yard?

Prudence realized it was a possibility.

The laird's furious expression rose in her mind. Since he didn't want her there, she might as well walk home. It was almost too good to believe but her belly rumbled again, which made Prudence frown.

There was no food in the forest.

And there was a great deal of forest to cover on foot.

The woman passed by the last worktable and started to walk into a passageway outside the kitchens. Prudence hastily grabbed up several items on the table. If these people considered that pilfering, so be it.

She would need the substance to survive the journey home.

The woman headed into the recesses of the back of the stronghold. Here, the stone was dark and there were no candles burning to illuminate the narrow passageways. The bustle of the kitchens was left far behind them, the sound of people being replaced with the howl of the wind.

"Get on with ye."

The woman had stopped at a doorway. She gave a huff and jerked her chin toward a door. So caught up in her idea of being freed to return home, Prudence walked through the doorway before she realized it didn't lead outside.

Instead, she entered a back storeroom. Prudence smelled the herbs that were hanging upside-down all over the ceiling. Every shelf was crammed full of newly harvested provisions. These were the medicinal supplies for the stronghold.

A door slammed shut behind her, and Prudence whirled around in time to hear a bar being slid across the door to secure it.

"Oh please!"

There was a snort in response to her plea. "Keep quiet or I'll send someone down to gag ye!"

Prudence stepped back from the door, clenching her teeth tight against the idea of being gagged again. She heard the woman walking away, leaving her to her fate.

Her fate?

Something snapped inside her. Prudence wasn't sure just what it was, but she was suddenly very pleased that she'd grabbed up the food. If she didn't fend for herself, she'd go without. That much was for certain.

So from now on, she'd have to take care of herself.

That meant escape, of course.

Prudence pushed on the door again, but it held. There were only small archer slits in the walls. The meager light they allowed in was diminishing. She turned around to investigate the storage room. Since she was stuck, she should eat and rest.

That way, she'd be ready when the door opened.

And she *would* be ready.

CHAPTER EIGHT

H IS FATHER NEVER raised his voice to his wife in public. But as Dugan drew closer to the closed door of his father's study, he heard his sire clearly.

"Are ye daft Alice? What do you think to tell me overlord to explain this action? When the earl hears ye sent Hay men across the border, he is going to be furious. Make no mistake about it!"

"I am making certain—" Alice argued.

"I know very well what it is ye want to make certain of, woman!" Laird Hay bellowed loud enough for the chickens to hear in the barn. "Ye want to saddle Dugan with a woman who will never be accepted by the clan! I have never demanded ye care for the boy, but ye go too far with this plan for him to wed an…Englishwoman!"

His father's personal retainers were on either side of the door. They moved into his path as Dugan headed straight for the closed door.

"This is one conversation I plan to be part of, lads," Dugan informed them in a hard voice. "Step aside now. This is a family matter, ye ken?"

The retainers weren't accustomed to Dugan taking a direct part in the running of the clan. But several retainers had fallen into step with Dugan on his way through the passageways and the men at his father's door stepped back rather than engaging.

Dugan pounded his fist on the door.

"Keep out!" his father bellowed.

Dugan opened the door.

"Forgive me, father, but I will be joining this discussion." Dugan firmly closed the door behind him.

His father scoffed. "Tis no a discussion. Me wife….will be learning that there are some things her so very fine blood can nae gain her."

His father stopped only because he needed to draw breath. Alice was set to argue with her husband, acting as though Dugan wasn't present.

"I will wed the lass," Dugan stated to bring his presence back to their attention.

His father turned around to stare at him, astonishment on his face.

"Ye see?" Alice was quick to swoop in and claim her victory. "Dugan understands—"

"I understand that ye—" Laird Hay faced his wife again. "—take advantage of the respect I have always afforded ye, no matter how much I disagreed with how harsh ye were toward my son!"

"The lass is here. Since it is Hay doing, we need to take responsibility for her," Dugan stated firmly. "I intend to wed her."

Alice preened. Cormac's eyes narrowed. He scowled at his spouse.

"I am not insisting that ye do so," Cormac said, looking straight at his wife. "Ye have not stained the girl's honor."

Alice narrowed her eyes. "The girl will be ruined, regardless."

"And it is yer doing!" Cormac slapped the top of his desk. He pointed at her. "Ye are a calculating bitch madam! Ye have made it so no matter what Dugan does, he will be labeled a blackguard!"

"When he weds the girl, his honor will be intact," Alice replied without remorse.

"But he'll never be able to become Laird of the Hay," Cormac snarled.

There was silence in the room. Dugan realized the moment

had arrived that he'd heard whispered about his entire life. Truthfully, he was looking forward to silencing those wagging tongues.

"I do nae want to be laird, father," Dugan interrupted. "It's better for the Hay to have a laird related to a clan such as the Sinclair. I see the wisdom of that."

His stepmother's eyes glittered with her victory.

Dugan fought the urge to tell her what he truly thought of her manipulating ways but for the first time, he had more than himself to think about. If he took Braylin as his wife, she would be answerable to the lady of the house.

To Alice Sinclair.

It would be best if he held his tongue.

Cormac Hay drummed his fingers on the top of his desk. "Ye are a fine man Dugan. I'm proud to call ye mine. And ye are me son. Ye will not wed an English girl."

"I did go to the bonfire and tempt fate by being the Laird of Misrule," Dugan said. "Truthfully, I did nae think beyond the moment of frivolity. As yer son, I was raised to be mindful of me actions, lest they bring shame to the Hay. I acted as a boy, and the lass has suffered for it by being torn from her family."

Cormac tapped the desktop with one finger. Dugan recognized his expression—his sire was thinking. And he realized that he had to claim what he wanted, for if his father spoke, that would be the way things would be. A laird did not go back on his words.

"I am going to wed her, Father," Dugan repeated very firmly.

"And if I do nae give my permission?" Cormac asked with a raised eyebrow.

Dugan felt his body tighten. "Ye've always told me facts matter less than appearances. What is said here will never outweigh what was told to all in the main hall. You will be judged as being soft with me on a matter of Hay honor because I am yer son."

And Dugan was going to have Braylin.

It wasn't mere anger that motivated him. This was something which went deeper, all the way to his bones. It defied his attempts to understand it. In fact, the only thing he seemed to be certain of was the way he recalled, in vivid detail, how Braylin's hair smelled.

And how much he wanted to bury his face in it again. To do that, he'd need to take the blessing from the Church, so that was what he would do.

"Alice, leave us," Cormac ordered.

Lady Hay didn't argue but quit the room quickly.

"Ye keep that fire hidden well, my son, yet I know it's in yer belly," Cormac declared before he poured whiskey into two cups. "Aye, ye're mine by Christ, and ye are a man now. So I'll tell ye plainly…ye do nae have to wed the English girl. The Douglases have a lass ripe for marriage. I'll get her for ye next spring. Best for ye to marry up…not across the border."

His father reached out and pushed the whiskey toward Dugan to seal the deal.

Dugan stepped back. His father inclined his head and lifted one finger into the air to indicate that he was adding to the offer.

"I'll send the English lass off with enough of a dowry to make her family forget about this incident," his father said, sweetening the deal.

"Honor is not bought, father," Dugan said quietly. "Alice planned well this time. The girl's family will nae accept her. This family has come to the moors because they will not compromise their values to maintain their positions."

The grin melted off his father's face, leaving behind a frank look which twisted Dugan's insides. His father didn't argue because he knew Dugan was correct.

"I've made me decision," Dugan stated firmly.

His father took a sip of his whiskey. It was a long moment of silence before Cormac spoke.

"We'll see if ye can get the girl to the church doors." Cormac grinned. "Have the whiskey, son, for ye've set yerself a large task.

One yer stepmother has made very difficult with her handling of the girl."

Dugan felt his mouth go dry. His father's words were full of hard, harsh truth. The sort of truth that most people could never overcome. He reached for the whiskey as something else surged through him—a burning in his gut that he recognized well enough. In his life, he had always had to work hard for anything he wanted. This would be no different.

He had no doubt that convincing Braylin to stand beside him and take the sacrament of marriage would be the hardest task he'd taken on yet.

CHAPTER NINE

"*T*HEY SHOULD BE *married immediately.*"

Prudence awoke with a start. The sight of the storeroom was rather comforting considering what she'd been dreaming about—Dugan.

So…wed him!

Prudence scoffed at her own folly. If she had any doubt as to how well life would go for her in a Scottish stronghold, the fact that she was locked in a storage room should drive reality home.

She needed to get away, and quickly.

The storage room wasn't pitch black. Around the edges of the arrow slits, she could see a faint glow of light, proving that it wasn't night any longer.

Yet it was still very early.

But she heard steps on the other side of the door. The staff was heading toward the kitchen, no doubt.

On impulse, she went to the door and knocked. Just a light tapping with her knuckles.

Time crawled by while she waited.

A few moments later, she heard another set of footsteps. Prudence knocked louder this time.

The steps stopped.

Elation flashed inside of her. Prudence rapped on the door again and was rewarded with the sound of the bar rubbing against the wood.

"Do nae nap in the storeroom, Una. Ye know it is always

locked at night. Serves ye right really, getting locked in."

The woman who opened the door didn't linger, or even look over her shoulder to realize that she wasn't talking to a lazy maid, but just continued on to the kitchens.

Prudence peered into the passageway, looking both ways before leaving the storeroom.

Her footsteps were loud, echoing between the stone walls, but there was nothing she could do about it. She headed away from the kitchens, looking for a way into the yard.

Laird Hay didn't want her wed to Dugan.

That meant Prudence might escape without fear that her family would be harmed. All she needed to do was be well away before anyone noticed she was missing. Given the laird's disapproval, she doubted Oran and his men would be sent after her.

She'd still have to face her father, of course, but she'd deal with that once she managed to escape the Hay stronghold.

Unfortunately, that escape was taking too long, and her steps were too loud. Was the sun rising impossibly fast? Prudence hurried down the next passageway, coming at last to a door. There was a row of hooks here with lengths of fabric hanging on them.

Nora had called them 'arisaids'.

Prudence took one, wrapping it around her head and shoulders. It would keep her warm and help her blend in better on her way across the yard.

Outside, the wind was brisk.

Prudence didn't let the temperature deter her. She went down the steps and across the inner yard where there was an opening in the wall with more steps leading down. Like all strongholds, the Hay castle was built on high ground.

There was ice on the steps. The morning light made it glitter. She started down them slowly.

"Ye are up early, Braylin."

Prudence jumped. The steps were narrow, which meant she

hit the back of the one she was on and ended up losing her balance, falling down hard on the one above. Her eyes widened as humiliation heated her cheeks. Dugan stepped in front of her.

"Take my hand lass," Dugan insisted.

His tone was low and soft, but he was impossibly large. He stared at her, clearly intent on stopping her.

"Your father does not want me here," Prudence said.

Dugan stepped closer to her. "It's cold lass. Let's go back inside. I will deal with me father."

Prudence stared at him, soaking up the details of his features which the night had hidden. He had dark hair and bright hazel eyes. He stood a full head taller than herself and was thick through the shoulders.

She shook off her fascination with him. "I should be going now."

His jaw appeared to tighten.

"Aye, ye should be going back inside, Braylin," Dugan informed her firmly.

Braylin. She'd been Braylin at the bonfire. Free. Unbridled.

"You shouldn't call me Braylin."

He raised an eyebrow. "Ye told me it was yer name."

"It was," she answered. "Yet not anymore. Such is my father's decree. We must both respect our fathers' decrees."

It was so hard to push her feelings down. They wanted to bubble up and be free, but there was also a stiffness in her neck from sleeping in the storeroom. She was not welcome in the Hay stronghold.

Prudence stood but Dugan blocked her path. His jaw was set, which only made her own determination flare up. She whirled around and went back up the steps. There was another way out of the inner yard on the other side.

Only she never made it there. Dugan scooped her off her feet, lifting her up as though she weighed no more than a child.

"What are you doing?" she demanded.

"Carrying ye back inside before ye catch yer death," Dugan

responded.

Once back inside the passageway, he lowered her to the ground.

"Are you going to lock me back in the storeroom?" Prudence demanded.

Maybe it would have been wiser not to give him any ideas, but her temper was hot and disappointment was fanning the flames.

"Who locked ye in a storeroom?"

If Dugan's jaw had been set before, now his expression was hard.

"I assure you, she did not introduce herself," Prudence replied tartly.

Dugan suddenly looked past her, and Prudence turned to discover a handful of women from the kitchen were in the doorway, watching.

"Braylin," Dugan announced, stressing her name, "is to be my bride."

"I am—"

Dugan returned his attention to her. "We can discuss the matter further in private."

In private? Prudence shook her head. "That is a terrible idea."

She wasn't afraid of him—not at all—but she was wary of the way she responded to him. If they were alone, she didn't trust herself to control her impulses.

There was a snort and some snickers from the women behind her. Dugan's lips twitched in response.

"Agreed, lass," he muttered softly. "Best to get a wedding blessing first, heh?"

Dugan shot a look past her at the women, giving them a dark look before he walked past her and disappeared.

ALICE WATCHED FROM her solar window as Dugan carried Braylin back into the kitchen.

She hadn't expected Cormac to champion Dugan. Perhaps she should have considered the possibility.

Alice felt her determination burning hotter. It was not temper, for the matter was not personal. She needed to make certain that Dugan would never be in a position to become laird. Such was the duty of a mother.

Alice smiled as she made another circuit around the solar. So many women looked at her and saw only the comforts which surrounded her. They never noticed the duty she labored to see done. Other women could be kind and overlook slights to their authority.

Not her.

Oh no, if she failed to demand her rightful due, she might find herself shipped off to a crumbling convent while her husband's mistress danced merrily in the great hall. She'd seen it happen to others. Even if Alice was willing to content herself with such a fate, she would never stand by while her children lost their positions. Her own mother had done the same for her.

Her husband's current mistress slept beside him. Alice felt her ire stirring in response to that fact, but she managed to tame it before her temper flared.

Fate had decreed that she'd been born the daughter of a laird. She knew, early on, that love wasn't something she'd ever be afforded in marriage.

At least, not love for her husband. It was dreadfully unfair the way men were allowed to enjoy the carnal comforts of affairs while their wives had to console themselves with scripture and the knowledge of judgements that would fall on them if they took comfort in a lover's embrace.

Alice loved her children deeply enough to fight for their futures. And she intended to give every last bit of strength she had to the effort.

Dugan was drawn to the English girl—that was a start. Alice

made another circle around the solarium as she plotted. Now, all she needed to do was find a way for the two to be brought together under the right circumstances. Just then, an idea blossomed inside her head. She strode across the chamber to one of her wardrobes.

She had just the thing to get Dugan to the church quickly!

CHAPTER TEN

"LADY ALICE SAYS ye're to make certain to come to the supper table."

Dugan turned around and stared at the young woman who'd spoken.

"Are ye simple, Erin?" Brody demanded. "This is nae a place for females."

The large yard beyond the old tower was full of men and youths training. There was the harsh, dull sound of flesh hitting flesh and bodies falling on the snow-covered ground.

Erin fluttered her eyelashes. "Lady Alice instructed me to bring her message to you myself. She said it was very important. I cannot consider the duty done by passing it to another. I must assure her that the message reached you."

Erin fluttered her eyelashes a bit more, and even added a pretty smile.

"What is wrong with yer eyes lass?" Brody stepped up closer to her. "Does the sun hurt ye?"

She let out a little sigh, then shook her head and left.

"That Erin is a strange one," Brody remarked. "I've never seen a female do that...fluttering her eyes like that."

Brody looked at Dugan, then frowned. "What is that grin about?" Brody demanded. "Are ye pleased to have yer stepmother sending her maid after ye?"

Dugan felt his grin growing wider.

Brody's eyes widened. "I don't understand you. Lady Hay

once again wants to have her way, and she is going to pester ye until ye bend to her whim. That's what this nonsense about coming to the supper table is all about."

"I know," Dugan replied.

Brody was still perplexed. "I do nae see anything to be so happy about."

"If the lady has gone to the effort of sending young Erin out here, the lass she keeps standing by her side the entire day long, I would guess that mistress Braylin will have also been told to appear."

For the first time in his life, Dugan was grateful to his step-mother.

It was an altogether new feeling for him.

Brody was frowning darkly. "Are ye still set on wedding that English girl?"

"I am," Dugan confirmed.

"She's tried to run off already," Brody added. "I've never been one for enchantments and spells, but something happened between ye two at that well, sure enough." Then, shaking his head and muttering under his breath, he went back to training the lads.

The Midnight Well...

Dugan would have liked to dismiss the idea of there being anything more to the well than fresh water, but considering the latest turn of events, he had to admit there might be something to the legend.

Enchantment or not, he fully intended to make Braylin his.

And tonight, they'd both be at the supper table, sure enough. Without a doubt, it would be a meal to remember.

BATHING IN WINTER took fortitude.

Prudence shivered but the household maids weren't taking no for an answer. Dugan had told the women that they were getting married, so she'd been taken straight away to the bathhouse.

"Go on with ye." A matron named Ryesen gave her a little nudge. "Closer to the fire. Ye do nae want to catch cold from yer wet hair."

Braylin clutched the robe she was wearing tightly as she moved over to the hearth.

"Sit down," Ryesen insisted. "Ye cannot dress until that hair is dry."

It was sound advice. Prudence's belly growled loudly.

"Do nae worry," a younger maid assured her. "We'll not be late to the table."

The young woman started to comb out Prudence's hair. Ryesen watched with a critical eye for a moment before she nodded with approval.

Someone rapped on the door. When they opened it, an older maid came in, her arms full of folded garments.

"Lady Alice sent this dress for the young lass to wear," the woman announced, placing her burden on a stool.

"My dress is very serviceable," Prudence remarked.

"And drab," the woman declared with a shake of her head. "Brown wool—the same shade as dirt. It's better suited for a nun."

"Vanity is a sin," Prudence said, squirming.

The older woman smiled at her. "So is being ungrateful… I suggest ye do nae turn yer nose up at the gift the lady of this house has sent ye from her own wardrobe."

The woman sent a stern look toward Ryesen before she grabbed Braylin's dress off the back of a table and headed for the door.

"Do not take my dress," Prudence protested.

The door swung closed in her face.

"Best to not quibble over the matter," Ryesen said softly. "Lady Alice is not one to be giving gifts often. Best to enjoy them when they arrive."

"Lady Alice sent men to abduct me."

The words were across her tongue before Braylin thought about them. The girl behind her froze mid-stroke. Ryesen stiffened as well.

"Would your family have ye back?" she asked.

Prudence wanted to say yes. She longed to be able to assure Ryesen of that. She even opened her mouth to answer before losing confidence in the matter.

Ryesen pointed at the girl combing Prudence's hair. The comb began sliding through the strands once more.

"We can only go forward," Ryesen declared. "Ye're clearly of the marriable age. Was there a match made for ye? One ye long to return to?"

Prudence shook her head.

"A match was recently been made for my older sister," Prudence answered truthfully. "We are less than a year apart, so naturally, I expected one to follow for myself."

"Lady Hay has seen to the matter now," Ryesen muttered firmly.

"Yet I am English." Prudence wasn't sure why she was arguing.

The maid pulled her hair with the comb, making Prudence wince. Ryesen winkled her nose.

"Dugan carried ye back inside himself. The matter is decided."

Something flickered to life deep down inside of her. The need to lift her chin and refuse to be cowed. "I do not believe it is decided."

Ryesen looked back at her, obviously noticing the glint in Prudence's eyes. The woman straightened and turned to face her. That flame was still burning in her belly and Prudence stared straight back at the woman, refusing to look away. Quite unexpectedly, Ryesen grinned.

"Ye have some spirit in there, after all. Well now, that is a relief."

It was by far the last thing she expected to hear...and it pleased her beyond measure.

DUGAN HADN'T THOUGHT he'd be nervous.

Yet he was.

It was not the first decision he'd ever made. Adult life was full of them. The challenging part was deciding what course of action to take, then being content with that choice. But when it came to wedding Braylin, he discovered it was not that simple.

If he were thinking with his head, he would have taken his father's offer of the Douglas girl for a wife. Such a bride would have raised Dugan's station.

But he wanted Braylin.

Wanted her more than he'd ever thought he might desire someone. Even knowing he'd owe his stepmother wasn't enough to worry him if it gained him Braylin.

"Stop grinning, if ye do nae fancy having yer cheek sliced," Brody snapped.

Dugan let his face relax as Brody scraped his face with a blade. His friend narrowed his eyes in concentration before he applied the sharpened edge to Dugan's skin and carefully drew it across the surface to remove any remaining stubble.

Dugan's heart was racing.

Yet it wasn't on account of the blade being used on his cheek.

"Well, ye do look good, I'll admit," Brody said as he stood back to admire his work. He reached up and stroked his own beard. "I hear the lasses like a clean-shaven man."

"Braylin is marrying me," Dugan said, pointing at his man. "So ye can just get that twinkle out of yer eye."

Brody paid him no heed but chuckled low and deeply. "She is a fine-looking female, but she did try to leave ye already once, lad. Have ye pondered that fact?"

Dugan felt his insides twist, but he shook off his doubt. "She snuck out of her father's house to meet me—twice—did she not?"

"No' precisely you," Brody argued.

But fate had decided it was him. Dugan recalled how hard it had been to leave her after the bonfire. The connection between them was too strong to ignore now that she was close again.

"I am going to wed her Brody," Dugan stated firmly. "I hope ye'll stand at me back."

Brody grew serious. He reached out and clasped Dugan on the top of his shoulder. "I will, man. It will be me honor to do it."

Someone began ringing the bells to summon the inhabitants of the stronghold to the hall for supper. Any man who didn't have duty on the walls would make a quick path toward the tables before the fare went cold.

Dugan was on his feet and out the door. It was time to meet his fate.

⇶⇷

PRUDENCE FOLLOWED RYESEN toward the great hall.

The passageways filled up with people making their way from the storage rooms and workrooms where they had been about their duties.

"That's her…"

"I hear she's a Puritan…"

It wasn't a surprise to find herself the main topic of conversation. Now that winter was upon them, any news would be a long time coming and anything new was definitely fodder for the gossip mills.

Prudence really didn't care. That flare of heat in her belly was still there, keeping her chin level. Even if it was strange to discover disobedience to be a source of courage, she wasn't going to lament it. She needed the strength too much to quibble over the source. The scent of food was tantalizing, drawing her forward. Honestly, she'd have gone to the great hall even if she'd worn naught but her shift. Her belly was empty and she suddenly realized how much she wanted to live.

Are you going to wed him then?

Prudence wasn't sure of her answer, only that she knew she would be pressed for one soon.

Very soon.

CHAPTER ELEVEN

THE HALL WENT silent when Prudence entered, much as it had when she'd arrived. Men toyed with their beards while they contemplated her with much the same looks she imagined they'd use on a hen at the market, while the women who were serving slowed to a standstill to stare at her over their pitchers and platters.

The dress lady Alice had given her was made of silk. It was delicate and ill-suited for anything except being presented. The garment was performing perfectly, making a spectacle of her.

Something snapped inside of her.

Let them look. She was too hungry to allow their silent judgement to keep her away from the table. Food had never smelled so good. Not even on a feast day.

The scents overwhelmed her, making her mouth water. Fresh bread. Hot porridge, which was different because it had oats in it. Fresh diced apples, and a pitcher of morning ale.

She could already taste it.

Prudence took a step toward an empty seat on a bench, but everyone was suddenly shifting and rising because the laird and Lady Alice had arrived. The men reached up to tug on their caps while the women lowered themselves into little curtsies.

"Be at yer ease," Laird Hay said, releasing them to return to breaking their fast.

There was another round of scuffling as benches and chairs moved on the stone floor. A retainer pulled back a chair for Lady

Alice, but she stood until her husband sat down. Laird Hay nodded, reached for his cup and drew a long sip of his ale.

Then he caught sight of Prudence. Laird Hay lowered the mug, his eyes narrowing. He swept her from head to toe before the sound of his mug hitting the top of the table cut through the conversation in the hall once more.

"That dress is ill-suited to winter weather," Laird Hay declared. "Ryesen, take the lass above stairs and get her dressed sensibly before I have to shoulder more guilt. 'Tis bad enough I have to suffer, knowing her parents worry about her fate."

Beside him, his wife bristled. "It is a most suitable dress for a wedding."

Laird and lady locked gazes. Everyone in the hall froze, waiting to see what the laird would say. Prudence was no different, for it was her fate that Cormac was about to decide.

"Winter is not the season for weddings, wife." Laird Hay's tone was congenial, unless one looked close enough to see the pinched look around his eyes.

"It is always a good season to see to honor," Lady Alice answered sweetly.

But no one missed the undercurrent of tension in the hall. Several retainers took to stroking their beards because it allowed them to cover their faces and keep their expressions secret.

"My son Dugan…" Laird Hay spoke slowly, to ensure that his words were heard clearly. "…has stated that there was no misconduct between them. I trust his word. There is no need for a hasty blessing since the girl is here and there is no worry she shall be cast out of her father's house into the grip of winter. As me son, Dugan's nuptials will be a celebrated event."

Lady Alice didn't argue further.

Laird Hay looked past Prudence and made a gesture with his hand. Someone immediately reached for her elbow.

"Come away now, the laird has spoken," Ryesen said, pulling harder when Braylin remained rooted in place.

She was starving…

She was so hungry, she couldn't think straight. But a second woman rose, making a little scoffing sound in the back of her throat, and together with Ryesen, managed to drag her out of the hall.

"When the laird speaks on Hay land, ye do as he says," the other woman grumbled. Prudence remembered her name as Niamh. "One would think ye learned that lesson last night in the storeroom."

Prudence's belly rumbled in response. Ryesen heard it, but she pressed her lips into a firm line, refusing to have compassion for Prudence's plight.

Whatever that snap of rebellion had been inside of her, Prudence suddenly realized that it had caused the dam of restraint to break, allowing defiance to flow through her. She pushed the first woman's hand down her arm. The action earned her an incredulous look from the maid.

"I have not eaten a true meal in three days," Prudence informed her. "Surely changing my dress can wait until after I break my fast."

"The laird has spoken—" Niamh pointed at her with a grim look on her face. "I'll push ye right out of this hall like a sheep if ye prove stubborn over the matter."

Prudence whirled around, facing off with the woman. "I've had quite enough of being pushed about by the Hay."

No one was more shocked than Prudence herself.

But it felt so very good to speak her mind.

"Is that a fact, mistress Braylin?"

It was Laird Hay who asked the question. So intent on the two women trying to push her out of the hall, Prudence hadn't noticed how quiet it had become. Once again, everyone was watching her, including Laird Hay, who stared straight at her from the high ground.

Well, let them stare!

Laird Hay was contemplating her. As master of the house, he most certainly expected obedience from her and yet, she simply seemed unable to duck her chin and give it to him.

"I warned ye, I did..." Niamh snorted. She came toward Prudence, her arms stretched out wide, as she might do if dealing with an unruly piece of livestock.

Prudence felt her body tense. The impulse to fight, something she'd had to quell when Oran stole her away from her family, suddenly flared back up. This time, she didn't need to fear her family members being cut down if she failed to be submissive. She'd never given in to the urge to fight in her life, but she wasn't going to be separated from the meal laid out on the tables without a struggle.

Jus as the woman made to charge at her, someone slid between them. Prudence ended up with her nose nearly pressed into Dugan's back.

She recalled his scent.

She straightened up, recoiling because Dugan's scent sent a flash of sensation through her. It was bright and intense, like lightning cracking open a black sky in the middle of winter.

Dugan reached behind him, capturing her wrist in a firm grip. The instant connection made her feel as if she'd been hit by a bolt of lightning. Dugan must have noticed her agitation because he stroked the inside of her wrist with his thumb.

The two women who had been trying to force her out of the hall shuffled back as Dugan began to walk back down the center of the aisle. He reached up and tugged on the corner of his cap in respect toward his sire and laird.

He'd surely heard his father's command.

Yet he turned and made his way toward a bench with enough space for both of them. Everyone was still silent, which meant that the bench feet scraped loudly against the floor when Dugan adjusted it.

Laird Hay was watching them. He was turning his mug around in a little circle, contemplating them. Dugan reached out, taking a round of bread from where it rested on a platter in front of them, tore a portion off and set it neatly in front of Prudence.

Laird Hay grunted, then turned his head, catching Erin in his sights. "Fetch the girl something to put over that dress to keep her warm."

Erin looked toward her mistress, but Cormac snapped his fingers at her. She jumped, dropping into a curtsey before she turned so fast, her skirt spun out in a circle, flashing her ankles and shins. Cormac glanced around the hall.

"The lass is no' the only one starving…" Laird Hay grumbled.

People resumed eating, the sounds of cutlery on plates rising up to fill some of the silence. Conversation was much slower to begin as everyone looked between the high ground and the place where she and Dugan sat.

Dugan continued to pluck items from different trays and put them on the plate in front of her. He didn't look directly at her though.

Prudence's cheeks were warm with leftover adrenaline after the scene she'd just caused, but she was far too hungry to do anything but eat. She reached for the food, feeling clumsy because she was moving too fast, but she couldn't seem to tame the need to stuff it into her mouth.

Dugan offered her a pottery mug, proving he was very aware of everything she was doing. That turned the heat in her cheeks into a full blush.

"Thank you," Prudence muttered.

Dugan turned his head and their gazes met. The connection she'd felt at the bonfire was still there, making her feel as if she was looking at a lost part of her soul. Dugan's eyes narrowed slightly, almost as though he felt the same way.

There was a scuffling behind Prudence, and he broke the connection to see who was arriving.

"Forgive me for taking so long." Erin was slightly out of breath, proving that she'd run most of the way. "If you'd stand, mistress…"

Erin held a sturdy looking surcoat, and proceeded to help Prudence put it on over her dress.

"It is almost a shame to cover ye up lass," Dugan muttered softly. "Summer seems a very long time away now that I know how truly fetching ye are when not swaddled up in dull-colored clothing."

Fetching…

Her cheeks were truly on fire now. Yet for the first time, she didn't feel any shame…even when Dugan motioned the maid away and buttoned up the coat himself.

It was overly bold.

And a statement of his claim on her.

Once he'd finished, he raised his gaze to hers. Prudence felt her world shifting. It was a level of intimacy she'd only ever shared with him. But this was no fleeting moment of frivolity that she'd walk away from and never return to. Dugan was making a very public statement in front of his clan.

Which meant the only way she was going to be free was to convince him to help her return home.

⟫⟫⟪⟪

ALICE LIFTED HER cup up to hide the way her lips were curving.

She would have preferred to control her expression, but she was simply too happy with the display Dugan was making.

It was perfect.

Beside her Cormac grunted, "Dugan! I have need of you today."

Her husband's voice bounced down the aisle to where his bastard sat. Dugan turned his head, reaching up to tug on his cap in response to his father's command.

But Dugan also turned and looked at the English girl before he left her side. Cormac growled softly beside her when he saw it.

Everyone else saw it, as well. That was the truly important part. Dugan was helping Alice to weave a net that would trap him into marriage with the girl. All Alice had to do was make certain an opportunity arose to push the two together.

An unexpected pang of jealousy hit Alice. She worried her lower lip, recognizing that Dugan seemed to be genuinely attracted to the girl. Caring for her just flowed naturally through him, unlike her own union which had always been awkward and forced.

She shook her head, reminding herself that pity wouldn't get her anywhere. Her parents had made a very excellent match for her and although her union lacked affection, her husband never slighted her in public. No, Cormac would save his personal remarks for when they were in private.

She was in a good place in life. And maintaining that state was something she had to keep up, eliminating any obstacle that might change the way things were. Luckily, in this case, altering Dugan's destiny was not all that hard....

THERE WERE SOME things which were the same, regardless of which side of the border a person was on. Prudence discovered that like any house, the Hay stronghold had numerous tasks that had to be dealt with, and since the winter days were shorter, everyone needed to pitch in.

Prudence had barely finished watching Dugan walk toward the high ground and his father before Ryesen came back, demanding Prudence follow her. It was time for them all to get to work.

Prudence went along contently enough, following Ryesen to a room where linens were kept. Here women were ironing the bedding, something that needed to be done carefully for cloth was expensive, and fine bedding overly so. Scorching it wouldn't do.

"Since ye've been fed, ye can earn yer earn yer bread," Ryesen informed her.

"This is not a work dress," Prudence argued.

"It will be a lot colder walk back to yer father's house in that silk." Ryesen pointed at the linens. "Or do ye prefer the storeroom as a way of ensuring that I do not have to suffer Dugan's ire when ye are found missing?"

Prudence glared at Ryesen, but the woman didn't appear to care. In fact, Prudence had a feeling that Ryesen would likely enjoy locking her in the storeroom again.

Prudence picked up a linen and laid it on the table, while Ryesen watched with a critical eye. Once she was satisfied Prudence was capable of doing the task, she moved on, leaving Prudence to deal with a large pile of sheets and cloths.

It was a strange sensation. The work felt familiar—she'd often done the same thing at her own home. But her mind kept reminding her that she should not be at ease where she was.

So where did that leave her?

Outside the snow had started falling. It was magical in its way, so pristine and crisp. It came down in thick clumps, covering the yard in no time. The silk dress would end up being her shroud if she ventured outside in it.

"Ye won't be smiling so happily at the snow in another few weeks," Niamh remarked.

Prudence turned to look at the woman who had tried to force her from the hall that morning. Niamh had her fists propped onto her ample hips, a look of malice in her eyes. But Prudence wasn't going to allow herself to be mistreated. She'd had enough of that already. So she fixed the woman with a steady look, refusing to cower.

"It is a fine sight when I have been working with a hot iron all day," Prudence said, hoping the woman would think she was settling in and no longer needed watching.

Niamh dropped a huge basket full of root vegetables onto the floor between them and sent Prudence a sour look. "Since ye find the snow so very pleasing, ye can take that over to the outer storerooms."

The other women working nearby suddenly all became focused on their tasks. No one wanted to venture outside the walls into the cold gloom of early evening while the snow was blowing.

Prudence looked back across the yard. There was an older, square tower there. "Where is the storeroom?" Prudence asked, needing better directions.

"Beyond the tower, go to the wall. Down on the far side, ye will see the door. Best get going. The light is fading, and supper will be on the table soon. Now that it is snowing, the head of house will be putting out less fare," Niamh added.

In other words, if she was late to table, she'd go to bed with an empty belly. Darkness was approaching too. The woman didn't seem to have even a smattering of shame over sending Prudence off into the evening shadows.

Perhaps there was a cloak or more arisaids in the storeroom…

Prudence bent down to pick up the basket, trying to hide her enthusiasm. If supper was on the table, and Dugan was still about the task his father had given him, she might well make her escape. The way the other woman had treated her only solidified her determination to leave.

The basket was heavy, filled with vegetables that still smelled like the earth, their skins still dusty from the ground they had been pulled from. In the last few days before the first freeze, there would have been a flurry of effort from everyone to get every last bit of harvest out of the ground before it was lost to the grip of winter's icy hand.

The kitchen and storerooms were nearly bursting with bundles and baskets like the one she carried. Now it was time for the women to sort it all, placing root vegetables such as these deep inside stone walls where they would stay nice and firm until needed.

After she went outside, Ryesen pulled the door shut behind her.

Prudence felt the snow crunching beneath her feet. Only the top was frozen, with powdery snow underneath—the sort that the wind could carry in white streams like the fall of petals in early spring.

But it wasn't spring yet, and the wind bit into her, finding the place where the collar of her surcoat was just a little too big for her neck and snaking down inside to chill her back.

Doubt nibbled on her resolve, but she shook it off. There would be something to wrap around her head inside the storeroom.

Prudence hurried toward the older tower, but the door was closed now to keep the heat in for the animals, forcing her to keep going around the corner and then along the side of it. Sweat popped out on her forehead and wet her hair at her temples but then the wind hit it and she shivered.

Once she emerged from the shelter of the old tower, she felt the full force of the wind. Somehow, it seemed as though it was blowing harder now that the light was fading. The darkness seemed to intensify everything that was so very normal during the light of day.

How many steps had she taken from the old tower?

How many left to go?

She squinted, trying to make out the wall. The wind blew full in her face, causing the moisture in her eyes to stiffen and freeze. This dress really was ill-suited to winter weather. When she'd been inside, she really hadn't noticed how thin the fine, soft blue silk was. Now the wind cut through it, making her feel as if she was wearing nothing but her shift.

And that powdery snow that she'd found so whimsical when she'd first stepped out into it was now coating her ankles, making her clench her teeth together to keep them from chattering.

Her footsteps crunched as she continued in the snow but finally, a few steps further, she saw the wall. Like so many stone walls, this one was darkened with time and the relentless weather. But at least she'd found it. She walked down the length of it, looking for the door.

When she finally found it, Prudence set the basket down so she could work the latch. It was stiff and sturdy, sticking tight when she tried to open it. By the time she'd managed to open it, there wasn't a hint of light left in the sky. Thankfully, she caught a glimpse of a candle left in a holder near the door.

With a happy smile on her face, Prudence reached into a little pottery dish sitting nearby for the striking stone inside. Her numb fingers didn't make the process simple but after a few strikes, brilliantly bright sparks fell into the little bowl to ignite the straw there. Prudence was quick to turn the candle over and hold the wick in the little flame before it died away.

Light was such a magical thing.

Prudence watched, letting out a sigh of relief as the wick caught, then brightened into a warm, welcoming flame. It cast a circle of light, showing her a space inside the walls. As she replaced the candle and picked up the basket, the wind blew the door closed behind her with a thud. She felt instantly warmer with the walls there to provide shelter.

Looking around, Prudence was thrilled to see piles of goods surrounding her. Everything she'd need to make her escape was there, and the darkness which had tormented her moments before now meant she'd be able to leave before anyone thought to look for her.

Hanging off a hook were more arisaids. She took one down and started to pile fruit into it.

She took a moment to wrap herself with the remaining arisaids before gathering up her bundle. Prudence muttered a quick prayer before she tugged the door open. Only to find Dugan standing there, looking at her.

CHAPTER TWELVE

PRUDENCE JUMPED. SHE whirled around, the bundle dropping from her fingers.

Dugan tilted his head to one side, appearing perplexed with her. "Are ye truly thinking to venture out in the darkness?"

Frustration drew its sharp claws along her hopes for an escape.

"Yes," she snapped. "You should let me go."

For a moment he appeared to contemplate what Prudence believed to be an uncrossable chasm between them. The differences between Scot and English felt so very great right now.

But he looked over toward a basket of fruit. He reached past her to pick up an apple. "Should I admit that I wanted to see what ye thought of me when ye looked into the water of the Enchanted Well?"

Whatever she'd thought he might say, that wasn't it.

Dugan tilted his head to one side. "I was drawn to ye, Braylin."

Prudence's mouth went dry. She felt exposed, because the truth was, she understood exactly what he was saying. She'd felt the same way.

Dugan held the fruit in the air between them. He pointed at her. "Ye did yer own share of enchanting me at the bonfire. The way ye looked at me with those dark eyes of yers. How could I resist?"

Braylin felt her eyelids fluttering. She had never felt

so…so…well, so very alive.

Dugan was watching her. In truth, he was staring at her with such intensity, she should have wanted to move away. But instead, she stared back, fascinated by the attention.

Time felt like it was standing still. Prudence didn't care what was happening outside of the storeroom. There was only Dugan and the way he made her feel. His gaze on her was intoxicating.

The semidarkness seemed to offer them permission to do…well, to be there together when it was something forbidden.

"Now that ye are here Braylin, I cannot fight the urge to keep ye," he muttered.

"That makes no sense." Her voice was raspy, sounding almost as though she was fighting herself with her protests.

"It does nae," Dugan agreed. "And yet lass, I want to see if ye tremble when I touch ye…as ye did at the bonfire."

Dugan lifted his hand. Prudence felt her breath catch in response. He was reaching for her, his hand coming closer until she felt the brush of his fingertips against her cheek.

Prudence sucked in a shaky breath.

She'd never felt anticipation, hadn't realized her body might react in such a way to just a simple brush of fingers against her skin.

She felt besotted by him, unable to look away. And she craved more of him. Much, much more.

Dugan didn't deny her. He leaned in, tilting his head to one side so that their lips might fit easily against each other. She shuddered at the first contact, pulling back to draw in a shaky breath that sounded abnormally loud. Dugan hovered near her for a moment, then pressed his mouth against hers once more.

His kiss was soft, gentle…and oh, so tempting. Her heart was thumping hard inside of her chest. She felt a rush of insane excitement, pushing her, teasing her. Prudence didn't know how to describe it—all she knew was she wanted more of it.

Dugan seemed to understand her need without her speaking. He closed the space between them, deepening the kiss. His hand cradled her face and his other arm was against her back, softly holding her against him.

As he slid his mouth across hers, teasing the delicate surface of her lips with his before increasing the pressure, a thrill of excitement surged through her. This was deeper and darker, but she didn't fear him. No, instead she was totally fascinated by Dugan, feeling as if she was being drawn deeper into the very heart of it. She could have stayed in his arms forever.

But moments later, Dugan lifted his head, severing the connection. In the darkness, his face was cast in shadows and the sound of his rough breathing filled her ears. Or maybe it was her own breath that she heard. Somehow, they had merged into one entity, making it difficult to know where she ended, and he began.

He smoothed his hand along the side of her face. "We'd best return to the hall where we do nae have privacy," Dugan said, his voice edged with frustration. "I do nae trust myself alone with ye. I believe this is going to be the longest winter of my life while I wait for our wedding day to arrive."

"I have not agreed to wed you," Prudence said.

One of Dugan's eyebrows rose.

"Do ye still mean to argue over the matter?" Dugan asked her softly. He reached out and touched her warm cheek. "Do ye not yet admit that we are very well-suited to one another?"

"Marriage is more than…reactions," Prudence replied, shocked at how husky her voice sounded.

He grinned. "Aye, it is. And yet, I believe we'll have a far better marriage because of the way we react to one another."

Prudence gasped. "Such bold words…" She struggled to admonish him even as she had to admit that his words excited her.

He opened his hands. "True words." He leaned toward her, making her breath catch. "Should I not speak the truth, lass?"

"Yes," she muttered almost too softly to hear. "But to be so brazen about something like this…" Words failed her.

His eyes narrowed slightly. "Not every couple reacts to one another as we just did. Have ye not worried over just who yer father would match ye with? I confess, I have spent a fair bit of time fearing the bride my father might choose for me." Dugan studied her for a long moment. "I never would have taken ye from yer home, but ye are here now. I will not let ye leave, lass."

"But I want to go," she insisted. "Why are you keeping me here?"

"Because you kissed me back, Braylin."

Yes, she had. All of her arguments evaporated when faced with that fact. She'd kissed him back, and she wanted to do it again.

It was wanton, and impulsive, and so very…Braylin.

"I am just as guilty of going to that Samhain celebration as you are. I know full well what me father would have preferred I do. And if we are confessing, I should not leave out the fact that I willingly snuck up to make certain ye saw my face in the water because I wanted to see yer cheeks turn pink. So…it seems the enchantment of the well has bound us both solidly to one another."

Prudence felt her eyes widen. "Spells are nothing to make light of, Dugan."

His face became serious. "Ye are no longer beneath yer father's roof, lass. The tale of the enchanted well was created by my countrymen so that no one builds a house next to it. Ye see, we need the water for our horses when we are crossing back and forth."

Astonishment held her in its grip. "You started the tale?"

"No me, precisely, but other Scots," Dugan explained. "It was a Scotsman who dug the well, so it seemed we should be the ones to use it. But since it is on English ground, well, a clever man thought of a way to keep the English away from it."

"That is…" Prudence struggled to find the right word to describe her feelings.

"What it is, is effective," Dugan informed her smugly.

"I suppose you're right. About the well, that is," Prudence said.

"So, we're back to the question of wedding." Dugan didn't dance around the issue.

"Your father does not like me," Prudence said. She felt her eyes widen. "There is nobody else here. You could help me leave. No one would know." Why had she not thought of it sooner? Braylin looked at Dugan, hoping he'd agree. But instead, she found him contemplating her with a serious expression on his face.

He shook his head. "Yer family and everyone ye know will consider ye ruined, Braylin."

He was correct—Prudence couldn't deny it. But she drew in a deep breath and looked him straight in the eye. "I will have to accept that as my just fate for being disobedient. My parents have spent a good amount of effort on trying to curb me of being impulsive."

Dugan crossed his arms across his chest, a small smile on his face—a smug smile. "I find ye to me taste, lass. Kissing ye should have proven that much to ye. I want to wed ye for more than honor's sake."

Part of her wanted to wrap herself up in his words. To simply be wanted, as she was.

It was so very tempting.

"Do not tease me, Dugan," Prudence implored him. "You have been forced to choose between your honor and being free of this scheme. I witnessed you being bent by Lady Alice."

A glint appeared in his eyes. "I've learned something new that I like about ye, Braylin. Ye do nae stand idle when injustice is being done to another."

The compliment was unexpected. Prudence discovered she liked it very much. But the knowledge that she'd be leaving made the moment almost bittersweet, and she surreptitiously studied Dugan, wanting to commit his face to memory.

One of his eyebrows rose. "Such selflessness is a fine quality to have in a wife."

"But Lady Alice is saddling you with a wife nobody will accept," Prudence exclaimed.

"Aye, it might take a while. But eventually, it will be well," Dugan agreed.

"Please take me home and free yourself," Prudence insisted.

"I doubt either of us will ever be free of one another, lass," Dugan said. "It seems the warnings about the power of the Enchanted Well are not groundless. We have both been snared."

When Prudence shook her head, Dugan suggested, "Perhaps we should test our reaction to each other again to see if wedding is a good idea or not." Then he caught her up against him in a motion that was almost too quick to register. One moment she was struggling to believe he meant what he said, and in the next, she was pressed against him.

If she'd felt besotted before, now she was entirely mindless.

Pressed against him from head to toe, she felt overwhelmed. His scent filled her senses, tempting her to curl her fingers into his clothing.

She wanted to hold him, as he was holding her.

It was an impulse far too strong to ignore. Fighting against it would have been like trying to rip off her own hand. Now that his mouth was on hers, the flame had caught. Holding back the flare of passion was utterly impossible.

This kiss was very different than their first one. His hand threaded through her hair, cradling her head so that he could hold her at the perfect angle. He knew what he was doing, moving his mouth against hers in a way that filled her with such intense pleasure, she felt as though her insides were twisting.

But she held him tightly, craving more of him. Beneath her fingertips, she detected the hard pounding of his heart. She pulled her head back...or tried to. The truth was that if he hadn't allowed her to move, his strength would have made her submit to him.

But he lifted his head, yielding to her will. She caught a flicker from the candlelight in his eyes which showed her his frustration.

"Did I hurt ye?" Dugan asked softly.

Prudence shook her head.

"Are ye frightened then? Is that why ye pull back?"

"I am…losing myself."

And she liked the way he felt against her. Words failed her as she flattened her hands on his chest, fascinated with how much she enjoyed feeling the warmth of his body against her own. No embrace had ever pleased her so very much. It was so tempting to allow him to do whatever he pleased with her.

He chuckled. "Be lost along with me, Braylin. I can think of nothing I desire more."

Dugan lowered his head, nuzzling at the side of her neck. A sound of male satisfaction rumbled out of his mouth before he pressed a kiss against her nape.

Suddenly, she felt a rush of frigid air. Prudence blinked, trying to focus on what had changed. Dugan turned her away from the door, placing himself between her and the two women who stood in the doorway.

Niamh had her hands propped on her hips. She stared at Dugan and Prudence before turning to speak to her companion.

"And here I was thinking this English girl had managed to get herself locked in the storage and needed someone to let her out."

The second woman made a little sound beneath her breath. "Seems the mistress is correct to get these two to the church doors for a blessing."

The pair of women turned and started back for the main stronghold.

"Wait—" Prudence started to argue but Dugan caught her wrist.

"Save yer breath lass. Ye should already have noticed that Lady Alice is very good at getting her way. My father put her in her place this morning, but it appears the lady is far from accepting defeat," Dugan said. "I stepped into her snare by following ye."

He sent her a determined look. "I am not sorry, for I plan to wed ye, Braylin."

At this moment, it was clear that Prudence was gone for good—she was Braylin again.

She only wished she knew how to feel about it.

CHAPTER THIRTEEN

LAIRD HAY WAS correct about the dress lady Alice had gifted to Braylin. The silk was very ill-suited to the winter weather.

Braylin shivered when Erin removed the loose over-gown that had kept Braylin warm throughout the day.

"No need to be so nervous," Erin muttered.

No, no need at all. It was odd how often weddings turned out to be happy events for everyone but the two people taking the sacrament.

Braylin felt a tug on her hair as Erin began to brush it out. The silence was so complete, Braylin could hear the sound of the comb moving through the strands. Erin opened her mouth twice before managing to think of something cheerful to say.

"The silk of the dress will glow in the candlelight. Ye will make a very fine picture on the way to yer groom. He is certain to be pleased."

Her groom…

Lady Alice had constructed a solid trap and now there was no escape. Braylin felt her temper flare. "I believe I have had quite enough of your mistress tampering with my life."

Erin gasped, then nodded. "I suppose ye have a valid point. But life is nae fair, especially not for women. We must take things as they come. Lady Hay will be yer mistress now, as well."

Her temper lessened. Erin was right.

"Dugan has forever been beneath lady Alice's thumb. Perhaps ye are truly a fine pairing and this wedding will finally satisfy the lady that her children's positions are secure," Erin offered.

"Secure?" Braylin asked. "How could such a thing be in question when Dugan is illegitimate and there is a legitimate son?"

Erin shrugged. "It's all well and good to have the blessing of the Church when a babe is born but a clan cannot be without a strong laird. If something happened to our laird, a half-grown son would nae be able to keep the Hay from being challenged. Why do ye think the laird keeps Dugan so close to his side?"

At Braylin's confused look, Erin continued. "Cormac took the lairdship because there was only a wee little lad in direct line when our last laird met his end. Lady Alice knows it well."

And the lady was using Braylin to secure her position. Braylin felt her temper stir again.

"Yer face is turning red. Best to make peace with yer temper," Erin admonished. "The way I heard it, ye and Dugan were getting along very well when the storeroom door was opened."

"Gossip is a sin," Braylin retorted.

"Kissing in the storerooms will be labeled one as well unless ye are wed," Erin answered knowingly. "It's best to not look at the details too closely. No one else will. Dugan will make a fine husband for ye and if there is someone back in England that ye had yer heart set on, best to look forward."

Because she was stuck in Lady Alice's trap. Braylin's cheeks remained warm but at least her temper burned away the sick feeling that had been threatening to turn her stomach inside out.

There was a solid rap on the door of the chamber. A moment later, Lady Alice entered. Braylin rose out of habit.

"Let me see you," Lady Alice instructed.

Braylin folded her hands together while the lady swept her gaze over her. "There are no flowers for yer hair, so I have brought ye some ribbon. Erin? Dress her hair quickly. The priest is waiting, and supper is ready."

Erin softly touched Braylin's shoulder, instructing her to sit again. The delicate silk of the dress she wore puffed out and settled around Braylin like a cloud. It also allowed a cold draft of air to chill her legs.

"Do you have any questions?" Lady Alice asked pointedly.

It took Braylin a long moment to understand just what the lady was hinting at.

The marriage consummation...

Braylin shook her head. Perhaps that wasn't the wisest choice she'd ever made for she truly had no inkling of just what was expected of her once the sacrament was given and she was left alone with her groom for the physical act that would complete their union.

But she refused to look to Lady Alice for mentoring.

"I see," Lady Alice clicked her tongue in reprimand. "You are not ignorant of the marriage bed. It seems you owe me a great deal of gratitude for making sure you are wed instead of just bedded."

"I am pure." Braylin stood up to square off with Lady Alice.

Lady Alice raised an eyebrow and smiled. "Pure? Ye went off to dance under the moonlight on Samhain. There is a wild streak in ye, no mistake about it." The lady sounded amused, and she wasn't finished. "Seeing ye wed to Dugan will solve a difficulty for me, hence I will overlook the fact that ye are English and not in good standing with Mother Church. Never forget that I am mistress of this house. Ye will answer to me, as will yer children and those who serve ye."

Erin was watching their conversation, wide-eyed and several Hay retainers stood by the door, looking on as well. Braylin's need to rail against the woman responsible for tearing her away from her family had to give way to the reality of her circumstances.

Lady Alice was the mistress of the stronghold.

And Dugan would not take Braylin back home.

No, he's going to marry you and bind you to this place...

Braylin lowered herself. In all her days, she had never fought so very hard to perform a curtsey. Every muscle felt taut enough to snap. Her jaw was clenched so tightly, she wouldn't have been surprised to hear a tooth cracking. She lowered her eyes to complete the picture.

They wouldn't know her thoughts though…

She heard a grunt of approval from the doorway where the retainers were still eyeing her intently. Lady Alice reached out and raised Braylin's chin so that their gazes met again.

"An excellent start." Lady Alice sounded like she was purring. She leaned in close and muttered, "Do yerself a favor and have a girl baby."

⇒⟫⟨⇐

"YE ARE FUSSING over him, Brody," Cormac Hay said, announcing his arrival with a critique.

Dugan reached up to tug on his cap. Cormac waved his hand, dismissing the need for a formal curtsey in a closed chamber. He squared off in front of Dugan, his gaze hard. But Dugan didn't look away.

"I will wed the lass, father," Dugan stated.

"My wife has already done enough to that little English lass," Cormac argued. "Ye do not need to wed her tonight."

Dugan drew in a deep breath. It wasn't his father who was making him impatient. No, the truth was, he wanted to stride back into the hall and take the blessing of marriage before anything interfered. But it appeared that the only one stopping him from claiming Braylin as his own was standing right in front of him. Dugan stood his ground.

"The lass will be shamed if I do not meet her in front of the priest," Dugan said. "And so will ye father, for all will say that ye are soft with me."

Cormac grunted. "If ye wed after that little bit of drama me wife just enacted, everyone will be saying how easily I bend to the whims of a shrewish woman."

"I want to wed Braylin." Dugan decided to finish the matter by admitting his feelings.

"And now my lady wife has made it easy to get that girl to meet ye at the altar," Cormac groused. "I would have found ye a better bride."

Dugan grinned. "I like Braylin, father. I hope ye will raise a toast to us." Dugan reached up to tug on his bonnet again before he turned around and went toward the hall where the priest was waiting.

"To me son!" Laird Hay raised his goblet high. The great hall went silent as the laird spoke. People grabbed their cups, raising them up to join the toast.

Braylin's throat was so tight, she couldn't even manage to swallow even a sip of liquid.

Because the ceremony was so sudden, the cook hadn't had time to prepare any lavish dishes. The head of house had tried to cover the lack of delicacies by opening several bottles of fine French wine. Braylin had her fingers laced around the stem of a goblet containing a generous measure of the dark brew.

Dugan lifted his goblet toward his father.

"Drink up, Dugan!" Cormac encouraged his son. "Refill the lad's cup!"

Lady Alice's eyes narrowed. She suddenly stood up. "It's time to take the bride above stairs!"

Cormac grumbled something against the rim of his goblet. Braylin didn't catch just what it was because Ryesen and others were pulling on her, taking her away from the high ground and off into the passageways that were lit only by candle lanterns, now that the sun had set.

Braylin stepped on the front of her skirt when they started up the stairs because the group was pushing her so fast.

"Do nae ye know how to raise yer skirt in England?" Niamh muttered crossly.

Somehow, Erin was there, popping up from between Niamh and another matron.

Erin took the lead, pulling Braylin through the open door of a chamber. The rest of the women followed, filling the space.

"Let's get on with this," Niamh declared. "Strip her down so we can inspect her."

Braylin's stomach lurched. Inspections were part of weddings. She knew it, even if she was unsure of just what would be happening later in the evening. The inspection though, Braylin understood.

Every inch of her was to be viewed by experienced women. To ensure she was unmarked by disease or deformities or by consorting with demons.

It was a necessary evil to protect her in the future should Dugan or his kin try to annul her union and keep her dowry.

Well, you have no dowry.

Still, the inspection was a wise thing to submit to. Being English, she didn't need to have any shadows that might be pointed out or gossiped about.

Braylin clenched her hands. The women took the layers of her clothing away until nothing was left. They even lifted her hair up to make sure they saw all of the skin on her back. The older matrons didn't draw the matter out, thankfully, but headed for the door, taking Niamh with them.

"Well, that's finished," Erin said cheerfully.

Erin held up a clean chemise, gathering up the sleeves so that Braylin only had to lift her hands and fit them into the openings. Then she dropped the soft linen garment over Braylin so that it fell into place.

They finished none too soon, either. Through the door they heard a ruckus on the steps. The men were coming up the stairs, their suggestions causing Braylin's eyes to widen.

They didn't knock.

Braylin stumbled back when the door burst inward. Erin sucked her breath, dashing across the chamber to grab an over-gown and return to drape it over Braylin.

The men's smirks told Braylin they'd all gotten a good look at her in naught but her chemise.

"Enough." Dugan's voice was hard with authority. Braylin stared at him, never having heard him commanding others before.

The men had obviously heard the tone before though. They all shuffled, averting their gazes. It didn't take them long to return to the spirit of the evening.

"Yer bride is ready for ye—"

"Ye are falling behind, laddie—" One of them tried to strip Dugan's doublet off him.

"Enough fun," Brody declared. "Get on back to the hall with the lot of ye."

The men went but not before they stripped Dugan down to his shirt, laughing and slapping him on the back before they quit the room. Brody paused in the doorway.

"Come along, Erin. Best to let these two sort matters out alone." Brody tugged the maid out of the chamber.

Braylin looked at her new husband. She belonged to Dugan now.

CHAPTER FOURTEEN

"I AM NOT going to pounce on ye."

Braylin snapped her attention back to Dugan. There was a slightly disgruntled look on his face.

"I didn't think you would," Braylin muttered. She intended to sound composed, but her voice was squeaky, giving her nervousness away.

Dugan tilted his head to one side; his expression made it clear he didn't believe her. Braylin took a deep breath and ordered herself to gather up some courage.

"I suppose it is only natural to be nervous," Braylin tried to explain. The problem was, she wasn't sure just who she was trying to convince, Dugan or herself. This time, she earned a node of agreement from him. He looked at her for a long moment, clearly trying to decide what he wanted to say to her.

"Rest easy lass, we do nae need to rush matters." Dugan had moved to the bed. "It's a fine, large bed. I'm sure ye shared a bed with one of yer sisters when the winter was bitter. Just close yer eyes and ye will never know it is me, and not one of yer siblings, beside ye."

Braylin blinked and then giggled. She couldn't help it. Dugan watched her, the corners of his lips rising up in response to her amusement.

"You are nothing like my sisters, Dugan," Braylin remarked. "Even deaf and blind, I could never mistake you for Modesty or Temperance. Never."

He grinned. "I admit I enjoy hearing ye say so."

"Truly?"

"Aye, Dugan confirmed. He held her gaze for a moment before he looked around the chamber. "I'll sleep in front of the hearth."

"We're expected to share the bed." Braylin was truly horrified to hear the words come out of her mouth.

Dugan turned back to face her, one of his eyebrows lifted. "Are ye inviting me into yer bed, Braylin?"

You did like his kiss. And you are wed now…

Her thoughts tempted her with the promise of once again experiencing more of the intensity that she'd found in his embrace.

Did she dare to say yes?

"Speak yer mind lass," Dugan encouraged her.

"Wives do not…speak their minds," Braylin argued.

"But you are *my* wife," Dugan said, "I would always have honesty between us."

Dugan waited for a moment before he continued. "I meant what I said about courting ye through this winter lass. Ye have no need to worry that I will be insisting on a consummation tonight. But I will nae say no if ye invite me into yer bed. The way ye kissed me back in the storeroom will nae leave me mind."

The memory was burning brightly in her thoughts as well.

There was a glimmer of anticipation in his eyes. Braylin felt something stirring inside her belly. A heat that made her feel restless. Those stolen moments inside the storage area were still burning brightly in her mind. The knowledge of how he'd opened some secret doorway inside of her, just begging her to celebrate the wedding night as it was intended to be.

No moment in time could be recovered once it was past. One had to live in the moment or risk living with regret.

They were wed….

Braylin looked at the bed. The covers were pulled back to show the clean, unmarked surface of the fabric. In the morning, the matrons would be back to inspect those sheets, looking for signs of her purity.

But that isn't why you want to invite him into the bed.

She fingered the bottom edge of her chemise. She didn't know what she felt—her stomach was churning, her breath was halted, and she was so very warm. Understanding what she was experiencing was impossible. But acting upon it, that would come easier.

"I would invite ye into the bed," she said.

"Are ye certain, lass?" He asked.

Was she?

"I am sure that I would like to be done with dreading," she admitted. "And I am certain that my future is here, with you. Our vows have been witnessed." Then she grasped the edge of her smock and lifted the garment up and over her head.

Dugan drew in a stiff breath. "Ye have courage, Braylin."

The compliment pleased her, easing some of the apprehension and leaving her with a prickle of anticipation. She locked gazes with him. Something shifted inside of her when she caught a glimpse of the mischief in his eyes.

Dugan reached over and pinched out the candle. The room fell into darkness, which suited her well, for she liked him cast in darkness best.

He pulled his shirt up and over his head. She watched him drop it over a bench before he came close to the empty side of the bed.

He was a creature of shadow and silvery glint—like the embodiment of every whispered forbidden tale she'd managed to overhear in the servant's kitchen. Her heart pounded.

She felt Dugan climb into the bed, making the bed ropes creak. He came close, so near that she felt his body heat. When he gathered her up in his embrace, she felt like it was all too much for her to endure but the moment he kissed her, she melted.

It was impossible to think. So she just sank into the heat and delighted in being held against him. A warm bed had always been a source of comfort. Now though, she discovered a much deeper sort of enjoyment between the sheets. It was far more intense than their kiss in the storage room, for now there was nothing between them.

"Ye are fair beyond my dreams, lass," Dugan muttered.

He gathered her close again, stroking her, kissing her. She tried to mimic his motions, allowing her instincts to guide her. The darkness was the perfect setting, for it heightened her remaining senses. Everything felt like it was building up to something…something explosive. When he pushed her onto her back, she clung to him, trusting him to guide her along the unexplored path.

There was a moment of tightness that became pain when he pressed forward into her. Braylin gripped his forearms as she gasped.

But it was gone a moment later.

Dugan was still, his length buried inside of her. She felt him kissing her brow with the most tender touches from his lips. A thousand honey-coated words couldn't have done as much to convince her of how enthralled he was with her in that moment. But the way he was still, waiting on her comfort instead of seeking his own pleasure was the most unexpected kindness she'd ever encountered.

For she knew that most men used their wives.

But instead, Dugan was soothing her.

She relaxed and he began to move. Suddenly her body, which had protested that first thrust, now felt as though she had been made just to be connected with him in the way they were now. A sensation of pleasure began to build inside her. She lifted her hips, moving faster until everything tightened inside of her. Pleasure burst inside of her like a bubble of pure light.

It was hot and intense, beyond anything she'd ever encountered. But she wasn't alone. Dugan's body went taut, and she heard him groan, while deep inside of her, she felt his seed filling her.

When he rolled off of her, she heard his labored breathing.

Her own heart was slowing down, leaving her relaxing more completely than she ever had in her life.

Well, if that was a wife's duty, she was pleased with her lot.

BRAYLIN WAS SLEEPING.

Dugan listened to the soft sound of her breathing. Her hair was a silky cloud. He touched it, smoothing some of it away from her face. He should sleep but his mind was churning.

He had a wife.

It was hard to believe, but more and more, he was fascinated by the idea. Everyone married after all. It was part of life. And yet, as he laid there, listening to the soft breathing of the woman beside him, Dugan had a hard time believing that the moment was real.

Perhaps he was drunk and would awaken to find the Samhain bonfire burnt down to coals and Braylin long gone.

Braylin shifted, and their knees touched. She made a soft sound before she turned away from him, seeking a more comfortable position.

Dugan followed her, securing her with one arm around her waist.

She was real.

And she'd clearly accepted their union.

At last, his mind stopped questioning the reality of the moment. But that left him struggling with a much larger quandary.

He had a wife.

In all of the time that he'd known he'd someday wed, he hadn't really thought about what he'd be able to offer a wife. He'd never had a taste for ambition, but now, he recognized that his choice would affect Braylin as well.

Tomorrow, he'd need to get on with finding a way to secure more of a position than just being the laird's bastard.

CHAPTER FIFTEEN

THE CHURCH BELLS hadn't yet rung when Lady Alice arrived the next morning.

The mistress of the house came by, with a full half dozen matrons at her back. Dugan growled at being awakened by the chamber door opening so early in the morning.

"Out of bed with ye both!" Lady Alice commanded.

Braylin struggled to open her eyes. She reached up to rub them before she recalled that she wasn't wearing a stitch. Her hair flowed down but it did little to cover her.

But no one was looking at her. She was shoved back several paces when the matrons all went to look at the sheet on the bed.

Erin had come in with the women, but not for the same reason. She found Braylin's shift. "Raise yer arms." Braylin let out a soft little sound of gratitude and lifted her arms so that Erin could help her into the garment.

"You spoke the truth," Lady Alice said, looking at Braylin. There was a pleased little smile on the lady's face. She pointed at the sheet. "Smearing a bit of blood on the sheets doesn't look the same as a true deflowering."

There were several nods from the other matrons. Two of them were pulling the sheet off the bed.

"Since ye are satisfied, might I ask ye all to leave?" Dugan's words might have been polite, but his tone betrayed his irritation.

Lady Alice looked his way. "Not just yet."

The matrons carried the sheet to the window. They opened

the shutters and tied the ends of the soiled sheet to them before they pushed the free end out of the window.

With the window shutters open, Braylin could see that the horizon was pink with the glow of a new day. The moment the sheet fell down, there was a cheer in the courtyard below.

The smile on Lady Alice's face faded. Braylin watched the way Alice's eyes narrowed slightly, seeing how many members of the clan had left their beds early enough to see the bed sheet flown. Dugan was clearly important to them.

Alice caught Braylin looking at her. A moment later, the lady abruptly turned around and left the chamber, with the matrons hurrying to catch up with her.

"They are gone," Dugan muttered after he firmly closed the door. "It's finished, lass."

The problem was, Braylin had a very odd feeling that matters were far from finished. There were too many voices in the courtyard.

And they were still cheering below.

Dugan's expression tightened. He walked over to the open window. When those below caught sight of him, they roared.

No, this wasn't finished. Because even in England, the master of a stronghold never wanted to share his position. Not even with his son.

"YE ARE IN a hurry this morning, Wife."

Alice froze when she heard her husband's voice. Cormac emerged from the shadows. The sound of cheering from the yard rose into a roar. Cormac made a motion with his hand which sent the matrons scurrying. He held his wife's gaze until the last of their frantic footsteps faded. Cormac closed the distance between them until there was but a single pace left.

"Ye are a fool, Alice," Cormac muttered. "Dugan is strong,

and we are getting old."

"She is English," Alice insisted.

Cormac scoffed at her. "Strength is life in Scotland. Or have ye forgotten that I took the lairdship away from a wee little laddie the same age as our Rohan?"

Alice shook her head, still determined to resist what her spouse was saying.

"Rohan has alliances because of my Sinclair blood," Alice argued. "I have suffered yer bastard looming over my son's position long enough."

"Is that so, Wife?" Cormac asked.

Lady Alice raised one of her delicate eyebrows. "It is, Husband. My son will be laird of the Hay. I have made sure of it." With that, she walked away.

Cormac moved over to a set of stairs, climbing a few until he could look out of one of the archer slits in the wall. Cold air blew in to chill his nose and cheeks but the sight before him sent an icy jolt through his heart. His lady wife was a fool to have so much confidence in her scheme, for the Hay were clearly not at all concerned over Dugan's parentage.

And his English wife wouldn't be the first to meet with an untimely, early death if the clan wanted Dugan to be able to make a more beneficial match.

Cormac let out a sigh. A moment had come that he'd often feared. But just as his young nephew had learned so many years ago, Cormac had a taste for power. And no one was going to take his position.

Not even his own son.

Alice was correct about one thing; Dugan had been in the stronghold too long. The Hay retainers knew him too well, and liked him too much. The benefit of having a son leading his retainers had now tipped too far in Dugan's favor.

Dugan didn't want the lairdship now, but once a man wed, he began to think of his legacy. Dugan would be no different. He would start thinking of ensuring a warm home for his children instead of riding the uncertain borderlands. And the Hay men were loyal to Dugan.

Cormac needed to remedy that oversight.

Immediately.

THE SUN WAS rising now, lighting up Dugan's face. He turned his head and caught her watching him.

Braylin suddenly recalled that she was in naught but her shift. She looked around for her clothing, but it was all in the far side of the chamber where the women had left it after stripping her.

"Are ye regretting yer choice, Braylin?" Dugan asked.

Braylin stopped halfway to her clothing and looked back at Dugan. He was watching her with a guarded look on his face. "Ye are running, lass."

He was right. Braylin opened her hands. "It is just that I have never been so undressed before a man...in the light of day."

Their gazes meshed. She fought the impulse to break that connection, not wanting him to think she was being dishonest.

"That is something we have in common." Dugan's expression finally softened. His lips curved up into the smile she recalled from their stolen moments at the bonfire.

That was all it took for her to forget about how awkward she was feeling. Once more, there was only him, and the way he mesmerized her, making her feel as though nothing mattered but the pair of them.

Dugan reached her, drawing her into his embrace. When he leaned down, her breath caught. This kiss was gentle and sweet. Braylin laid her hands on his chest and felt his arms tighten around her in response, but Dugan broke away from her.

"Day has broken, lass," he muttered, his expression serious. "I needs get to the task of being a husband."

His words warmed her. The sensation was wholly unexpected. Then Dugan left the chamber, affording her a moment of privacy to smile.

Perhaps the future would be bright, despite the way they had come together.

It could be, if you get dressed and figure out how to be a worthy wife.

Her inner voice was spot on. Without a doubt, there would be challenges waiting on the other side of the chamber door for her to meet. She was still English and it was unlikely some of the keep's women had changed their opinion of her.

Well, as Dugan had said, the day had begun. The Hay were about to learn that Braylin was finished being their captive.

"YE SENT FOR me, Father?"

Cormac looked at his son across the expanse of his desk. There was a tightness in his body that he recognized, for it was always present when he needed to perform a necessary task that didn't sit well with him.

"Aye, I did."

Cormac watched his son reach up and tug on the corner of his bonnet. It pleased him that Dugan made certain respect was paid. The two retainers in the room needed to see that Dugan kept to his place, even in the privacy of the laird's solar.

"It's time for ye to have position within the clan," Cormac stated. "I have decided ye will have stewardship of Black Moss Tower and command over the retainers who call it home."

It was a gamble, giving Dugan a command, but the distance to Black Moss Tower balanced it out. The main body of Hay retainers wouldn't see Dugan every day, and therefore, not be able to compare his merits to Cormac's.

Cormac pushed a small leather pouch toward his son. Dugan picked it up, withdrawing the signet ring inside. Cormac had thought long and hard over giving his son this token of his trust, but knew it was the right thing to do. The ring would declare Dugan's new position as master of the tower.

"Father, I am honored," Dugan said.

"Put it on and wear it with my blessing. And may you have a long stewardship in service to the Hay clan," Cormac said.

Dugan looked at the signet ring for a moment before he opened his hand and pushed it down onto his finger. This was the seal of authority. It would be pressed into wax on letters and documents.

"I will strive to be worthy," Dugan said solemnly.

Cormac locked gazes with Dugan. "Ye shall leave immediately, in hopes of beating the full strength of winter. Yer retainers are already waiting for ye in the lower stable."

Dugan hesitated for a few seconds, then reached up and tugged on his cap once more. It seemed to Cormac that his son hardened right in front of him. Dugan had always been mature, but now, Cormac saw something glitter in his eyes, marking the final transformation from youth to man. His kilt swirled up and away from his thighs as he turned and quit the room.

Cormac was still for a long time. He'd always thought he'd have no trouble paying the price for being a laird. But it had never stung quite so badly before.

Still, every man needed to rise to the challenges of life. Dugan would be no different. If he wanted more from his life, well, Dugan would have to carve his place out just as Cormac had done. It was time for Cormac to see just which of his sons was more worthy to follow him. And to discover that, Cormac decided to follow the lead of the ancient Spartans—he needed to put Dugan out of the stronghold to see if he could survive.

The look in his son's eyes promised Cormac that Dugan intended to thrive.

BRODY WAS SHOCKED.

Dugan appreciated the moment because Brody wasn't a man who was easily shocked. Dugan pointed at the feathers on the side of Brody's hat.

"Ye can raise one of those up now, since ye will be me captain at Black Moss Tower," Dugan said.

Brody only continued to stroke his beard. "It will be a hard journey."

"Aye, it will," Dugan agreed.

Black Moss Tower was strategically placed at the edge of Hay land where the sea had eaten away at the rocky landscape to form a peninsula. Sitting on the high ground, it housed messenger birds which could be sent to the main stronghold.

But it was much further north and on the coast. They'd be riding straight into the breath of winter.

"Yer father is putting ye out—" Brody didn't mince words. "—to protect his position."

"That's one way to look at it," Dugan agreed.

Brody titled his head, clearly not seeing any other way to view their situation. But in his father's solar, Dugan had felt something shift inside himself—almost as if a door had opened in front of him. For certain he didn't know what was on the other side of it but a sense of anticipation had started flickering inside of him. Brody squinted at him, clearly baffled by Dugan's lack of concern.

Dugan looked at his man. "It is an opportunity to be my own man, Brody."

Understanding dawned on his friend's face. "Aye, well the Lady Alice is likely none too pleased to hear of yer new position."

"Aye," Dugan agreed. "But I am happy to be heading to a place where I can stop roaming the borderlands."

Brody took another long pull on his beard before he sniffed and nodded firmly. "Ye've earned it, lad," Brody declared. "I'll gather the men. You go collect yer wife."

His wife.

Would Braylin go with him? He wasn't sure. Trust was something that took time and they'd had precious little of that, as of yet. He knew she had courage. But riding out of the gate and into the unknown was asking a lot of even the strongest of men, much less a woman who had been torn from her home. He hoped she'd face the challenge with him because there was no way he was leaving her behind.

CORMAC KNEW EVERY inch of his stronghold—every stone passageway, even the ones which ran into the outer walls. To have a place inside the walls was considered a luxury, or at least better than a croft on the lonely fields in the dead of winter when all you might do is huddle close to a fire fed with peat.

But to be inside the walls meant a person needed to provide some service in return. The stronghold needed all sorts of labor—from the retainers, who stood watch on the walls and promised to put themselves in harm's way if needed, all the way down through the kitchens and laundry, to the meekest of servants who cleared out the privies.

In the outer walls, there were store rooms and bunks allotted to the lowest level of servants. Cormac headed into one of them, surprising several of his people who blinked with astonishment to see their laird so far from the great hall.

Cormac knew who he sought and just where his lady wife had banished her to. At the back of the walls, where they joined, was a space with four bunks. It should have been rustic and lacking in luxuries, but when Cormac made it to the doorway, he was greeted with warm light from several pottery lanterns. And there was the scent of beeswax instead of tallow from the candles. On the rough stone alcoves which formed the bunks, he could see thick pallets to make soft beds and there were pillows and other items which made for quite the cozy dwelling.

The occupants turned toward him, their faces lit with smiles of welcome until they recognized him. Fear replaced that welcome in a flash as the three women backed away from him. He knew any other man would have been made most welcome, in the hope of him purchasing their favors. But no one wanted to risk offending the mistress by bedding her husband.

Cormac looked at the three women. They were all fair and well-groomed. He paused inside the doorway, tapping a cake of fine soap that was sitting on a wash stand.

"It would seem ye are all doing very fine business."

Two of the girls' pallor turned pasty white but one of them looked him straight in the eye. Cormac immediately dismissed the other two. What he needed was boldness. "I require a service of ye, mistress."

Then he looked at the other two. "I was never here."

They both ducked their chins in obedience. "Aye, me lai—". The fact that they managed to bite off the word 'laird' before finishing pleased him. "Go, and do nae listen at the door, or I will have ye taken to the convent."

The two girls hiked their skirts and ran without a backwards glance.

"Yer men will be very displeased should ye put us out, Laird Hay."

Cormac chuckled. "Ye have a sharp tongue."

The girl's eyebrow rose. "I assure ye, me tongue is very soft and subtle."

She came toward him. Cormac felt as though his shirt collar was suddenly too tight. There was a look in her eyes which mesmerized him, but she stopped short of touching him. Instead, she reached over to pick up the cake of soap.

Cormac cleared his throat when the woman lifted the soap to her nose and drew a breath.

"I know ye have a mistress already, me laird, so what brings ye here?" the woman asked pointedly.

Cormac felt a prickle of irritation over the woman's lack of respect but he shook it off. She was precisely what he'd come looking for.

"Being direct is likely a good trait in one of yer profession," Cormac stated bluntly. "What is yer name?"

The woman sat the cake of soap aside. "My name is Leana, me laird. Life afforded me a father who settled his debts with my maidenhead. After that, me sire bound me in servitude to a brothel owner who gave him a percentage of my wages. Now that I am free of that arrangement, if someone wants a service from me, ye had best be ready to pay a fair price for it."

Cormac reached into his doublet and withdrew a small leather coin purse. Leana's gaze went to the purse, her expression turning pensive.

"Me son Dugan is heading out to Black Moss Tower. I want ye to join his party as a laundress and when the moment is right, get caught in his bed by his new bride."

Leana's face became a smooth, unreadable mask. But in her eyes, Cormac could see that she had no liking for his request. Never in his life had he ever thought that he'd have to convince a whore to do his bidding, but this was more than just paying a fee for the use of her body. He needed her wiles.

Life had a way of humbling a man when he least expected it.

Cormac opened the bag and slowly emptied the contents onto the spot where the soap cake had been. Leana drew in a swift breath, obviously noting that the coins were gold instead of silver.

"Assist me in getting this English girl to leave on her own and I will give ye twice as much upon yer return."

Leana didn't jump at the offer. Cormac lifted a finger into the air. "If you succeed, I will send ye to Lindsey land with a personal letter so that ye can begin a new life far away from those who know yer past."

Now there was a different look in Leana's eyes—hunger.

Aye, she was hungry for a better life. It was only natural. And no one else could give it to her except him.

"The English girl is innocent," Leana argued. "She was forced to come here."

"I am not asking ye to harm her," Cormac continued. "Get her to abandon me son and go home." He pointed at the gold. "Give that to her as a dowry. Mange the matter before the next full moon and ye will go to Lindsey land with enough gold to live as yer own woman or wed as ye please."

Leana looked at the gold again.

"How do I know ye will keep yer word, me laird?" Leana asked. "I can hardly walk into the hall and demand justice."

She was weakening. Cormac felt the victory coming to him— he just needed to sweeten the deal a wee bit more.

"Ye were correct when ye said me men would be displeased if I sent away yer companions. Why do ye think I have never interfered with yer commerce?" Cormac shook his head. "If I did nae understand the value ye bring to me stronghold, ye can be very sure I'd question just how one of me wife's French soaps made it here."

Cormac wasn't really giving Leana a choice. If she refused him, there would be no further business within the walls of his stronghold. Understanding dawned in her eyes. There was a hint of bitterness there, but she nodded in agreement.

"Good." Cormac pointed at her. "Dress yerself and hurry to the yard."

At that, Cormac turned and left the chamber. He shrugged off the guilt that suddenly settled on him. He was just getting the English lass to go home. Other lairds would have sent some to break the lass's neck.

He surely hoped it wouldn't come to that.

"I WILL SEND ye back to the scullery if ye do nae pay attention to yer duties, Erin."

Alice watched Erin jump, whirling around and ducking her chin when she realized Alice was looking at her.

Alice let out a soft grunt. "What could be so interesting in the yard?"

Erin lifted her head, her wide eyes glistening with unshed tears.

"Well, Erin?" Alice pressed for an answer. "What is happening in the yard?"

"The laird is…is sending Dugan to Black Moss Tower," Erin finally squeaked out a response.

Alice was stunned, blinking a few times as Erin's words sunk in.

"That cannot be," Alice declared. She stood and moved over to the window, pushing the shutter further open so she could lean out and get a good view of the courtyard below.

Erin had spoken true.

Dugan was there, along with a full three dozen retainers—far too many men for it to be a matter of Cormac sending Dugan on some errand.

"Erin, go down there and see if the laird has given Dugan the signet ring," Alice ordered.

Erin didn't need to be told twice. She grabbed her skirt and took off. Alice returned to look at the yard below, watching as Dugan was confronted by one of the older retainers. Dugan extended his hand to show the man the proof of his new authority.

Alice let out a profane word.

She paced across the chamber and back, trying to decide how to keep Cormac from elevating Dugan's position in the clan. But the signet ring was already on the bastard's hand. It was something which could not be undone and the news of it would spread through the clan, taking precedence over Dugan's wedding to an English girl.

Cormac was clever indeed. He'd managed to think of a way to throw a bucket of water onto the flames of the scandal she had so very carefully crafted.

She'd have to be cunning in return.

Erin came back into the chamber. She was out of breath and stood for a moment huffing and puffing. "He has the signet ring, Mistress."

Alice paced some more, trying to think of a countermove. Finally, she turned and looked at Erin. "You are going with them," Alice said.

"Mistress?" Erin questioned with wide eyes.

"Yes." Alice liked the idea the more she thought about it. "You are going with them to Black Moss Tower. And you are going to keep me informed about everything that is happening."

Alice hurried over to her wardrobe, withdrawing a small key from her belt, then fitting it into a chest that was inside the cabinet.

"This is a signet that the master of the mews will recognize." Alice handed over a small disk to Erin. "Keep it hidden, Erin, and tell no one of our arrangement. I expect you to write me a letter every week."

"Mistress, everyone knows I work for you," Erin protested.

Alice sent Erin a scathing look. "I do not have time to find someone else I trust. Think of a way or I will wed you to one of those dung shovelers in the stables before the week is out."

Erin's face twisted with horror. Alice grabbed the girl's hand and slapped the signet into it. "Hide that in yer bosom, girl."

Then Alice went into the small alcove where Erin slept. She grabbed the girl's worn surcoat and gloves.

"Here," Alice said, tossing them at Erin. "Get down to the yard before they leave."

Erin hugged the clothing to her chest, worrying her lower lip. But the stern look on Alice's face quickly had the girl hurrying from the room.

Alice went back to the window, watching for Erin to emerge at the bottom of the tower. When she did, Erin had donned the surcoat and was wrapping an arisaid around her head and shoulders. Alice smiled in approval. With the Hay colors covering her head, Erin easily blended in with the handful of women who were making ready to depart with Dugan.

Cormac wouldn't win this game.

Not while there was breath still in Alice's body.

CHAPTER SIXTEEN

B RAYLIN DISCOVERED A new appreciation of her plain brown wool dress along the road toward Black Moss Tower. Lady Alice's gift dress would never have held up against the bitter wind. Even the livery Ryesen wore was of a finer grade of cloth and better suited to the inside of the Hay stronghold. Ryesen had a long piece of wool wrapped around her shoulders that she called an arisaid. Even so, Braylin could see that the chill of the encroaching winter cut through the fabric.

Braylin leaned over, trying to shield her fingers. The Hay retainers all had sturdy gauntlets to keep their hands warm.

The horses didn't start the journey eagerly. The animals snorted and protested being urged toward the gate. Braylin pitied the creatures, for they had no say.

Neither do you...

Well, she'd had her say the day before. A flicker of heat rose in her cheeks. Braylin welcomed the blush, refusing to shy away from the memory of the way she'd willingly wed Dugan...and invited him into her bed.

At the time, it had seemed right. Of course, in the light of day, reality wasn't nearly as nice. She looked around at the people joining them on their trek to Black Moss Tower. They were all being put out—because of her.

Braylin wanted to think of Dugan's new position as a good thing but the looks being cast her way from the Hay retainers made it clear they thought she'd brought disaster upon him.

Seeing the way Ryesen shivered, Braylin found the joy she'd experienced the night before dissipating. Their future wasn't going to be simple.

Her temper stirred at last. Even if she understood that life wasn't fair, it seemed to her that both she and Dugan had received their allotment of unkindness.

But what she thought didn't matter. Dugan had married an English girl. If she'd come from a powerful bloodline there might have been some measure of acceptance, but she was a common girl without even a dowry to ease her arrival into the Hay clan. And they were both paying the price for it, she thought, as two more of the Hay retainers glanced her way, disgust on their faces.

Braylin suddenly sat up straight. She tightened her grip on her composure and earned a raised eyebrow from one of those men watching her. She would not be weak in front of them. Braylin swallowed her doubts and looked toward the open gate.

Dugan lifted his hand, giving the signal for them to ride out of the yard. He never looked back, so she wouldn't either.

BLACK MOSS TOWER was ominous.

Braylin was bone weary and half frozen and still the sight of the fortification made her wish they were just going to ride past it.

It had three towers, each one of a different height. The center of it had a roof as well, which formed a hall to gather and break bread in.

The fortress was set on the edge of a ravine. The tallest tower overlooked the gaping canyon that looked like a huge beast had just taken a huge bite out of the earth. Behind half of the tower, there was a cliff with more exposed boulders and ground. There was a set of steps cut into that cliff because on top of it stood another lone tower.

The stone was black with moss. Wind howled up through the ravine, carrying rain that made that moss glisten.

"It is fearsome lass, but that will ensure ye feel safe within its walls."

Braylin had been so absorbed with looking at the towers, she'd failed to notice that Dugan had ridden up beside her.

Her husband…

She found it hard to use the word still, but it made her tingle when she thought it.

Dugan smiled at her. "We'll make it a fine home. I saw ye working on the flax linen, Braylin. Together, we will build a fine life here."

Dugan was eager to begin. He kicked his horse and went riding up to the front of the line of retainers. All of the horses were picking up the pace now that the animals could see an end to their journey.

"Only a fool would see this place as something to celebrate…"

The words floated back to Braylin from a cart in front of her where six women huddled together on top of what appeared to be sacks of provisions. The ride was bumpy, and a pair of retainers had to walk behind the cart to shove it forward when the wheels got stuck in ruts or against rocks.

The men were splattered with mud and debris, the scowls on their faces making it plain how dissatisfied they were with their duty. The women rolled and swayed, their fingers digging into the ropes which crisscrossed the sacks of grain to keep from being tossed over the sides.

"The bastard has never had anything of his own…"

"And this will be his lot, so long as he keeps that English wife."

Braylin looked back up toward the towers so the women wouldn't know she'd heard them. Part of her wanted to look straight at them and refuse to be upset by their words.

But there was another part of her that ached because she

knew there was truth in what they said. All of her wishes meant nothing against the immovable hatred between Scot and Englishman. Henry VIII had wed his own sister to the Scottish king in an effort to unite the two countries, yet here, on this rocky road, there appeared to be no softening of hearts. She might have borne it if it was just herself but it would affect Dugan, as well.

She'd become an anchor weighing him down.

THE BED WAS warm.

Braylin shifted closer to the source of heat, catching the scent of Dugan's skin.

Heat stirred in her belly.

Somewhere between slumber and waking, she couldn't resist the urge to nuzzle against him. That flicker of heat inside her grew. Dugan obviously felt it as well, shifting and stroking her. Every place where their skin met produced pleasure on a scale that simply overwhelmed her.

Lost in the extremes of her reaction to him, she could only sigh when he pushed her onto her back and filled her body with his. The intensity of the moment built, becoming a wave that rushed toward the shore. When it broke, pleasure rushed through her and left her clinging to her partner.

"Och, lass, ye tempt me to hurkle-durkle with ye," Dugan said against her temple. He pressed a kiss there and drew in a deep breath.

"Hurkle-what?" Braylin asked.

"Hurkle-durkle…lay about and do naught," Dugan answered her. "Except please myself and ye!"

She opened her eyes to take a good look at him. This was an intimate moment, to be sure. His hair was tousled and there was three days of whisker growth on his chin. He reached up and ran his hand over his unkept chin.

"Another thing I need rise and attend to," Dugan muttered.

There was a groan from the bed ropes and then a draft of frigid air when Dugan lifted the covers and left the bed. He grabbed his shirt and shrugged into it.

Braylin averted her eyes, and took a first real look at her surroundings. The night before she'd been so tired and cold, she'd eaten a bowl of hastily prepared porridge and climbed into bed.

Now she could see that the chamber had cobwebs in every possible place. Dust was so thick on the tops of the other furniture in the chamber, she wouldn't have been surprised to see a plant spouting out of it.

There were baskets and sacks and piles upon piles reaching all the way to the roof line in places and now that she was completely awake, she caught the scent of moldy food in the air.

Dugan had finished pleating his kilt and belting it around his waist. He stood and caught the look on her face.

"You are not the only one who cannot be lingering in bed," Braylin muttered.

She heard a chuckle from him before he turned and grabbed his bonnet on the way out of the chamber.

Hurkle-durkling?

Well, there would be none of that for a very long time!

THE MEWS WERE on the very top of the rise at Black Moss Tower.

Erin shivered on her way up the step stairs, tucking her skirts up because they kept getting in the way. It seemed an impossible distance, but she finally heard the birds. Their calls came from the lone tower on the top of the hill. When she made it to the base of the structure, the sound of the animals was much louder.

"What is yer business here?" a voice greeted her when she opened the door.

The man who tended the mews was huge. Scars decorated

his face and hands—long scars from swords or knife blades and other round ones that might have been made by spikes.

"Close that door, girl."

Erin was frozen in terror. The man growled, reaching over to grab a handful of her arisaid. He tugged her inside and firmly shut the door. There was fluttering above her and several disagreeable squawks.

The man pointed up. "Birds do nae fare well in the cold."

The tower itself was rather wide. The floor was covered with rushes like her grandmother's home had been. Above her head, where the roof rose into a cone, there were dozens upon dozens of branches stuck into the walls. Birds perched on many of them, their eyes bright.

There was a sound of exasperation from the man.

"Yes," Erin said, recalling her purpose. She produced the signet disk.

The man's eyes narrowed. He took a long look at the disk before he grunted and extended his hand. Erin gave him the tiny scroll that she'd written her message on.

"Don't let the heat out when ye leave," he ordered.

Erin knew she'd been dismissed but she did linger long enough to see the man look up. He seemed to select a bird, letting out a whistle. A moment later there was a flutter, and the bird came down to perch on the man's shoulder. He reached into a pouch hanging from his belt. Some of the other birds began to cry out when he did it but the food he withdrew was offered to the bird on his shoulder.

"Eat up now, ye have some work to do," the man cooed. He sent Erin a side glance. "Get on with ye girl. I do nae need yer mistress accusing me of trifling with ye."

Erin went back out into the cold weather. But the wind was not what made her shiver. No, it was the sinking feeling that by being obedient, she'd somehow committed a grievous transgression.

Hay stronghold

CORMAC LOOKED UP from his desk. One of the retainers who guarded his study had entered, followed by another man—the master of the mews, who wore a leather hood and collar around his shoulders.

Cormac gestured for the man to enter.

"Another letter from Black Moss Tower so soon?" Cormac asked as the man tugged on his cap in respect.

The man cleared his throat. Cormac squinted at him. "Spit it out, man."

The man reached into his jerkin and withdrew a letter. "It's from Black Moss Tower sure enough, me laird but…it was sent to Lady Alice."

Cormac shot up out of his chair. He grabbed the letter, nearly tearing the tiny scroll in his impatience to see what was written on it.

His wife had planted a spy in Dugan's party.

Cormac snorted with disgust, but there was something else burning in his gut too—satisfaction. He was going to enjoy dealing with his wife.

He found Alice in the great hall, another girl standing uselessly behind his lady wife in case Alice needed anything.

"I warned ye Alice. I warned ye to leave Dugan be," Cormac said, reaching his wife.

Alice looked up just as Cormac tossed the scroll at her.

"You forced him to wed that English lass, and I put them out, but ye are still not content!" Cormac didn't care who heard them. "Ye are a selfish bitch, Madam."

"I am protecting Rohan's rightful place," Alice declared.

His wife was on her feet, squaring off with him while members of the clan watched. Cormac knew his men—and the maids from the kitchen—were all edging closer to make sure they didn't miss a single word.

To be the master of the house, he had to put Alice down.

"Dugan is my son." Cormac spoke slowly to ensure his words did not run together. "He will have a share of what is mine. Ye were told that the very day ye arrived to wed me, Alice."

"Name Rohan yer heir, and me as his Regent, and I will leave yer bastard be," Alice demanded.

"Why sort of fool do ye think I am?" Cormac asked incredulously. "The moment I seal such a document, yer kin will send an assassin down here to help me into me grave."

Alice jutted her chin out. "I will accept nothing less."

Cormac shook his head. "Ye are selfish, Alice, to deny Dugan a place of his own."

"He is bastard born," Alice growled. "My father would never have sent me to wed ye if ye had not agreed to give my children everything. I have royal blood in my veins."

Cormac took a moment to think about that. His wife did come from a very well-connected family. Such a thing had been important when he'd wanted to take over the position of laird, and now, he had to deal with it. She knew her worth and wouldn't be bridled easily. While such a trait was desirable in his son, in his wife, well that needed to be managed with an iron grip.

"Ye are greedy Alice, and it pains me to see how consumed ye are with material possessions." Cormac shook his head again. "Ye had that English lass brought here against her will. Dugan wed her to please ye, in spite of knowing I would have made my son a far better match but…." Cormac lifted his finger into the air. "Ye are still not content with how much ye have taken away from Dugan. Now ye have a spy in his house."

"Bastards have no right to anything," Alice countered.

"Well now, if I were to leave the boy with naught, that would be ignoring my own part in just how the lad came to be here," Cormac argued. He heard a few snorts from his men. "A laird can nae shirk his responsibility, not ever. Dugan is due a place in me house."

"The place he wants is to be laird." Alice declared. "Well, I have seen to it that he will not have what is rightfully Rohan's."

Cormac held up the scroll. "Dugan has already wed the English girl. Why did you feel the need to put a spy in their midst?"

Cormac was baiting her. And now, Alice was too far gone in her rage to consider how her words might sound to those listening.

"Because I need to know if his seed takes root," Alice declared with a huff. "Yer bastard cannot have a son. I will not allow it."

There was more than one gasp in response to Alice's words. Cormac held his tongue, allowing her words to ring through the hall. Alice's eyes widened, obviously recognizing her mistake. She looked past him, her face turning red when she saw just how many people were watching them.

"Alice, I am fearful for yer immortal soul. It is the duty of a married woman to produce children. Ye are the one who insisted on them being wed," Cormac said at last. "In the morning, I will have ye taken to the convent for the winter. I hope ye will cleanse yerself of this obsession with greed. It is a bad example for our children."

His wife's eyes narrowed, but Cormac simply turned and walked away. Several of his retainers were boldly standing there, making no attempt to hide the fact that they'd been listening. Cormac made sure to appear concerned when he passed by.

The chill in the air suddenly pleased him. He was going to enjoy having the winter to indulge himself with his mistress without his wife there to bother them.

"Don't think I'll be minding a word that ye say."

Braylin admitted that her patience was wearing thin. She fixed the newest Hay woman who was intent on disliking her before they were even introduced with a firm look. The head of house of Black Moss Tower was a round woman wearing an apron with dozens of splotches on it. She was eating what appeared to be a piece of sweet bread with jam glistening across its top. She bit into it and chewed with loud smacking sounds.

Braylin realized she wasn't just low on tolerance; she was completely out. She reached out and grabbed the piece of sweet bread from the woman.

"Here now!" the head of house exclaimed. "Taking the very bread from my hand, are ye? Just like the English!"

"How dare you serve my husband and his men naught but thin porridge two meals in a row and keep such a fine treat for yourself." Braylin held it up when several of the Hay retainers turned toward her, ready to defend one of their own. But they stopped short when they looked at the piece of sweet bread. A couple of them actually sniffed the air and licked their lips when they caught the scent of the jam.

"I didn't know ye were coming," the head of house said, defending herself.

"Do you mean to say that Laird Hay gave Dugan the signet ring, but failed to send a message here?" Braylin questioned. "Let me ask the master of the mews if there was a scroll delivered."

The head of house jutted her chin out in defiance. "Alright...there was a scroll, but the Lady Alice made it plain what allotment a bastard and his English slut were to be given."

"I am not a slut," Braylin growled.

"I understand ye crawled into that bastard's bed quick as could be! Yer parents must have been relieved to be rid of ye...English slut!"

Braylin saw red. For the first time in her life, she understood the meaning of the word 'rage'.

It flared up inside of her so intensely, she didn't have time to think. She lunged toward the portly head of house, intent on clawing her, but never made it even a foot. Someone grabbed her dress and yanked her backwards.

Braylin turned to find one of the retainers looking at her with a bored expression on his face.

And jam in his beard.

"Shavon is the head of house here and Lady Alice is the mistress of the Hay," the retainer informed her before his tongue made a swipe along his upper lip. "So get on with ye and stop making trouble."

Don't give up.

Braylin really wanted to heed her inner voice, but she was at a loss as to how to proceed. She looked at the floor and saw a bucket. It was full of water and looked like a gift from heaven. Braylin stooped down, picked it up, and tossed the contents into Shavon's face.

Shavon let out a scream, the sound bouncing between the walls of the hall. There was a stampede of footfalls in response. Those who had been beyond the hall or in the yard came running, thinking there had been some accident.

Instead, the entire household skidded to a stop when they realized who was facing off with whom.

Shavon was sputtering. Her face was red, and she opened and closed her mouth, looking like a freshly caught fish.

"I do hope washing your face helps you see clearly," Braylin announced, then turned to look at those watching. "Perhaps the rest of you need to wash your eyes out as well, so you can see how much food she keeps for herself and her friends." Braylin looked at the retainer who had a wide waist. "While the rest of you get naught but porridge."

"English…"

"Meddling…"

The inhabitants of Black Moss Tower weren't going to go against one of their own, even if they were a pitifully thin bunch.

Just then, Brody arrived, having obviously heard Shavon's scream. He came forward, his expression promising Braylin nothing.

Dugan was impressive but his man Brody was hard. There

were scars on his thick forearms which attested to his less-than-easy life. Brody stopped beside the retainer in question. He fixed the man with a hard look before poking him in the belly.

"Ye eat well…very well," Brody announced. He looked at Shavon. She scrunched up her face and opened her mouth, but Brody cut her off. "Far better than I have beneath this roof."

"I am the head of house!" Shavon declared. "Lady Alice is me mistress."

Brody looked at her. "If ye want to remain in yer position, I suggest ye wipe yer eyes and look closely, for there is a new master of Black Moss Tower. I do nae think he will take kindly to unfair treatment of any of the people who honestly toil to serve this house."

Shavon shut her mouth. Brody looked around, locking gazes with everyone watching. When he came to Braylin, he paused, then reached up and tugged on the corner of his cap. "Mistress."

CHAPTER SEVENTEEN

S HAVON PUT A decent supper on the table.

Braylin received many looks of gratitude from the retainers who had traveled with them. She might have remained in the hall to enjoy them but with her belly full, keeping her eyes open proved impossible.

She climbed up the narrow stairs which went along the edge of the tower. Round and round she went until she stopped in front of a chamber door. Inside the room there was still a fair amount of dust, but at least the moldy smell was missing.

Against the wall, half of the baskets and sacks were gone now, taken below to have their contents sorted out. Shavon had collected more black marks against her ability to manage the house when Braylin had discovered the source of the musty scent was food that had gone bad while stored.

"Ye spent the day well," Dugan said, surprising her by arriving right after she did.

Braylin spun around to find her husband looking straight at her. He closed the chamber door but never broke eye contact.

"There was much to do," Braylin answered. But that was all she said. Shavon would not turn her into a weak-willed soul who couldn't face her own challenges.

Silence stretched out between them. Dugan finally let out a frustrated sound.

"A wife should come to her husband with troubles, Braylin," Dugan informed her gruffly.

Braylin started to nod, but she ended up looking at the closed chamber door. He raised an eyebrow.

"I dealt with the matter," Braylin told him.

The words were out of her mouth before she could think. Then, suddenly—joyfully!—she realized that with Dugan, she was free to offer her opinion.

But when Dugan's face tightened, she wondered if she was wrong.

"Ye are my wife Braylin," Dugan chastised her. "When someone attacks ye, it is an attack upon me."

"Shavon did not touch me," Braylin said, defending herself. "In truth, I threw water on her."

Dugan crossed his arms over his chest. "Ye are skirting the issue. She challenged yer authority and denied ye the respect due yer position."

"True respect is earned," Braylin answered. "I do not care to live a life that is naught but a façade. Better to have Shavon speak her mind so I know who I need to look out for."

"She called ye a slut, Braylin." Dugan wasn't going to let it go.

"But there was a proper supper on the table. Shavon's words will only incriminate herself now that your men have been given their fair measure." Braylin smiled smugly. "Words will not hold up against full bellies."

Dugan contemplated her for a long moment. "I'd have rather ye came to me, Braylin." He closed the space between them, leaning over her, seemingly intent on impressing his will upon her. She started to argue with him but then looked again at the closed door, and catching his scent, she reached up and locked her hands behind his neck. His eyes widened and then hers were closing as she tilted her head to the side so that she could press her mouth against his.

Dugan groaned.

As far as compliments went, Braylin had never enjoyed one more.

Or felt her confidence grow so much in response.

She kissed him with every bit of that newfound confidence, moving her mouth against his and marveling at the sensations running through her body.

Dugan lifted his mouth from hers. "Ye are trying to distract me, Braylin."

Braylin pressed up against him and felt the bulge of his hardened cock. "If you think I will come to you with tears in my eyes, you should haven't have encouraged me to act like the girl you met at the bonfire."

His eyes narrowed but his lips thinned in a very sensual way. "Is that the way ye see it?"

She nodded firmly. "If anyone is going to run crying to you, expect it to be Shavon. I shall not waste my time alone with you on nonsense. There are much more enjoyable pursuits for us to engage in when the door is shut, and our duties finished for the day."

A glint appeared in his eyes. "There surely are." Then he scooped her up, cradling her against his body and carried her to the bed.

Hay stronghold

ALICE SAT IN front of her looking glass—a fine item that had been brought in from France for her wedding. She smiled softly, enjoying the proof of just how powerful a match she had with Cormac.

There would be no cloister for her.

Just as Cormac was laird of the Hay, she was the lady of the stronghold and she had done her duty in providing a son.

A legitimate heir.

Noble wives who went to nunneries were the ones who had failed in their primary duty. Men had enough power in the world.

They shouldn't be able to send a wife who had done her duty to a cloister.

A new maid was carefully pulling the copper hair pins out of Alice's hair. The girl set them aside, paying attention that none of them fell onto the floor to be possibly lost. Alice waited for her to brush out her hair. On the table in her room, there was a thick candle marked for each hour of the night. A quick look confirmed that it was now late into the evening.

"You are dismissed, Eda."

Eda's lips curled up into a satisfied smile. She inclined her head before hurrying to the door and quitting the room before Alice changed her mind.

The only person changing their mind tonight would be her husband.

He wouldn't do so easily.

But Alice had to admit, she did enjoy the challenge her spouse presented. No victory was worth celebrating if it was handed over without a struggle.

She moved over to where a tapestry hung on the wall. She pulled it up, slipping behind it and into a passageway which ran up and down the tower. The steps were narrow and the stairwell tight. It went up between the outer wall and the interior walls of the main stairs, cleverly hidden there in case the occupants of the upper floors needed to escape.

Or in this case, sneak into the laird's chamber.

There would be a pair of retainers in front of the main entrance of Cormac's chambers and of course, her husband knew of the secret passage. But Alice doubted very much that Cormac had stopped to consider just why she never took issue with the fact that his mistress occupied his bed every night.

Alice reached the next floor. She pushed on the tapestry that covered the opening, slipping into the room. It was cold, but then, she was only wearing a shift. She caught sight of the long hair lying on the pillow next to Cormac and heard her husband snoring.

Perfect.

Alice moved across the chamber, stopping beside the bed. She tapped the girl on the shoulder gently. Her eyes fluttered, then she opened them up, blinking a few times before focusing on Alice. The girl's face betrayed her fear over seeing her lover's lawful wife standing next to her.

Alice gestured for the girl to follow her back across the chamber. Alice held the tapestry up so that the girl could slip into the narrow stairwell. "You will sleep in my bed. Do not rise until a full hour past first light. Remember your mother and sisters all work in this stronghold and they answer to me." Alice pointed down the steps.

The girl was worrying about her lower lip, clearly debating the wisdom of crying out to wake Cormac.

"Has my husband promised ye that he will elevate yer position now that he thinks to break my spirit by sending me to a cloister?" Alice asked in a whisper. "He cannot leave me there for long. My family would question the matter. Whatever place he gives you, I will push you off it when I return. And it is a very long way down, I promise you."

The girl drew in a stiff breath. "I am obedient, my Lady," she said, her hand settled over her flat belly. "I take the….concoction every day. It makes me ill."

"Of course it does, it is poison. You cannot have the laird's favor and children of your own. Not in a place where I am mistress."

The girl nodded. "I take it, Lady."

Alice smiled to soothe the girl. "Which is why your family enjoys a fine life. Your nieces and nephews are being taught to read. Think of the bright future ahead of them. They will be more than just scullery servants. Mind me now."

The girl looked past Alice, toward Cormac, longing glittering in her eyes. Alice was jealous once again, but this time, she harnessed the strength of her emotions to use it for her cause.

"He is my husband, and I am the mother of the next laird of

the clan," Alice informed the girl firmly. "I have no quarrel with the place ye have in his life, so long as you do not grow outside your boundaries into what is mine. Dugan might seem congenial and kind, but all men enjoy power. He will think to taste it at some point and then both you and I will be swept aside when he takes the lairdship. An English bride will prevent that, preserving the life you and I enjoy. As a wife, I must protect my husband's place, even if my husband does not see the need for it."

The girl bent beneath the weight of the truth. Alice watched her turn and start down the narrow steps. High or low born, they shared their gender and women had to be clever to carve out their places in a world run by men.

No one had everything. Some had love. Others enjoyed a high position. Alice turned and retraced her steps across the chamber. Beside the bed she drew her smock up and over her head, leaving it on a stool. She lifted the bedding and slipped beneath it to settle in beside her husband. Cormac would discover he was no different than anyone else.

Truthfully, she was rather looking forward to the look on his face when he realized she was in bed with him.

Cormac groaned as he woke.

He stretched out his legs and felt his cock tightening. In the predawn light, he caught sight of the back of his bed partner's head on the pillow next to him. He rolled over, gathering her up in his embrace while thrusting forward to find release between her thighs.

"Awh…" Cormac groaned when his cock sank into her.

The bed rocked with his thrusting. He pushed his partner onto her belly, rising up behind her and grasping her hips. Need swept through him, driving him faster toward that pinnacle of release.

He cried out when his seed started to flow. His fingers gripped her hips hard to hold her in place so that his seed might find a place to take root. That was instinct, of course. In truth, he knew his wife made sure his mistress did not conceive.

One bastard was enough.

Dugan ensured the Hay didn't look around for a successor while Rohan was growing up. Dugans's wedding to an English girl was a bit of a problem but such a thing could be managed. Cormac smiled as he thought of Leana. The English lass would be gone in short order and Dugan would be well on his way to earning the respect of the retainers at Black Moss Tower.

Cormac would have preferred not to have given Dugan the signet ring, for it made it clear Dugan was his choice as successor. He had considered letting his son leave without it, but then, Alice and her meddling needed to be quelled.

There was a rap on the chamber door. His men would not have allowed the servants in until they knew the laird was ready to have company.

Let them wait on his pleasure; he was the laird.

"Enter!" Cormac called out.

The double doors opened instantly. Two neat rows of household servants came in with their arms full of items. Cormac stretched. His back popped. His personal servants reached him, one of them holding out a basin. He extended his hands so that another servant might begin pouring warm water from a pitcher over his hands. A scent of rosemary rose from the water.

"My lady," someone gasped from behind him.

Cormac turned to look back at the bed. Where he should have seen a maid helping his mistress into a dressing robe before the girl was taken to the chamber beneath his to be attended to, he saw Alice standing there, looking straight back at him.

There was a glitter of victory in her eyes. Alice made sure he saw it before she held her arms out for the dressing robe.

"Everyone out!" Cormac roared.

There was a mad dash for the doors. The two retainers who

guarded those doors even grabbed the shoulders of the last servants to reach them and pulled them out of the chamber so they might answer their laird's command that much faster.

"Ye…Ye…." Cormac sputtered, his complexion darkening.

"Would ye really have the mother of yer heir be a simpleton, like your mistress?" Alice asked honestly. She moved over to a small table where one of the platters of food had been placed. She took her time selecting something to enjoy before she looked back at her husband.

Cormac appeared to be contemplating her words.

Or her fate.

"You cannot send me to the cloister now, Cormac," Alice said, deciding to voice what he was so obviously attempting to find a way around. "For the bloodline of the laird must be unquestionable. Everyone knows you bedded me. Ye cannot send me away until I bleed, and by then, winter will truly be here."

Her husband's eyes narrowed, but she'd won, and she knew it. She looked back at the platter and selected another piece of food, making a little sound of enjoyment when she bit into it.

"Ye are so very pleased with yerself, Alice." Cormac spoke at last.

Alice lowered the piece of fruit she held because there was a hint of anticipation in his tone, one she recognized, and knew to be wary of.

Cormac smiled at her. "I agree with ye, Wife."

Alice frowned, trying to decide just what he was hinting at. Cormac didn't leave her suffering ignorance for long.

"The laird's bloodline must never be in question," Cormac announced softly. "Ye will not journey to the convent for if ye are with child, I will know without question that it is my babe."

Alice felt a shiver touch her between her shoulder blades.

She almost made the sign of the cross over herself but managed to quell the impulse. Still, Cormac could likely read the trepidation shimmering in her eyes.

The wide smile on her husband's face confirmed it.

"Ye left my bed years ago, Alice, I respected yer wishes. But now that ye have returned, I will perform me duties as yer husband."

Cormac's expression became one of warning. "Ye will remain here in my bedchamber, under my personal supervision, until ye bleed. Just as ye decided it would be, madam. Since ye have decided to gamble, I will ensure ye see it through. There will be no concoctions to ensure ye bleed. Only my servants will attend ye." He looked closer at her. "And don't think about using the secret entrance. That will be guarded as well."

He pulled on a shirt and walked to the chamber door. "Open!"

When the retainers complied, her husband left without looking back at her.

"Close it!" Cormac commanded his men and the door shut with a hard bang.

Alice shivered. She had won. For now.

Black Moss Tower

BLACK MOSS TOWER didn't have a high ground for the master table to sit upon. The modest hall provided the most basic of benches and tables for the retainers to eat at. One table was turned longways to denote it as the head table.

"Sit beside me, Braylin."

Braylin frowned, for it seemed as if Dugan was speaking louder than normal. But it was early, and she confessed that there was still fog clouding her thoughts. Behind her, she heard the scraping of the benches being set down on the stone floor. During the night, they were stacked high on top of the tables so that the retainers might sleep in the hall.

Off to one side, several of them were still laying the pleats of their kilts out on the floor before they laid down and used a thick belt to secure it around their waists. The moment one stood up, another man was there with his length of wool that had served as his bedding during the night.

The staff was bringing breakfast in from the kitchen. It was a simple meal, meant to help everyone begin the day's chores while the main meal of the day was produced. There was bread to turn and savory dishes to prepare.

The inhabitants of Black Moss Tower were chosen because they could defend it. All else came secondary to the needs of the tower's defense. And with only the towers and the hall for shelter, there were very few women. Braylin turned to go and help bring in the pitchers.

"Ye are the mistress of this hall, Braylin." Dugan was definitely raising his voice. "The staff will serve ye. Sit beside me."

Braylin stared at her husband.

And she was not the only one.

Around them, the hall grew quiet. She heard her heart thumping hard inside her chest.

Sitting felt impossible. But her husband had spoken.

Off to one side, Shavon stood with her lips mashed into a snarl but two other maids hurried forward to begin serving Dugan and the place where he wanted Braylin to sit. They both looked at the ground, their shoulders hunched in submission.

Braylin turned and started to leave. But Dugan caught her. His fingers clamped around her wrist, pulling her to a stop before she'd traveled even half of the passageway length.

"I will not have ye called a slut, Braylin," Dugan declared. "Why do ye flee from my effort to treat ye as a respected wife?"

"Because I do not want to be like Lady Alice," Braylin replied.

Her response seemed to make him pause.

"You did not see the way the maids hunched their shoulders in fear," Braylin explained. "I do not want a place that is enjoyed at the suffering of others. What manner of life is that?"

"This is not just about you, Braylin." Dugan wasn't going to relent. "I wed ye. This refusal to acknowledge ye is a judgement of my choice."

And he'd had no choice under Lady Alice's rule.

But Dugan suddenly looked toward the end of the passageway. "Erin?"

Braylin turned her head and saw Erin, Lady Alice's personal maid frozen at the end of the passageway.

Dugan let out a word in Gaelic that Braylin didn't need translated to understand it was a curse. Dugan looked back at Braylin, pointing at Erin.

"Ye are kind Braylin, but yer compassion will only serve my stepmother's desire to destroy any future we might build here. This is our house and yet Lady Alice has sent instructions for me men to be starved and a spy to report every going on here. Ye will sit at the table tonight and be served as the mistress of Black Moss Tower. The staff will make their choices. Anyone who doesn't choose us, will be put out."

CHAPTER EIGHTEEN

NO BRIDE COULD wish herself back to being a maid again.

Braylin felt guilty for even thinking the question, but she couldn't seem to stop her mind from churning. Of course, she was practical enough to understand that she and Dugan knew very little about one another, so conflicts were going to occur.

Yet she could not seem to stop thinking about it.

"Yer face is as dark as thunder clouds."

Braylin was startled. She jumped and spun around to see a woman carrying a sack into the storage room. She placed the sack on a shelf before she dusted her hands together.

"I am Leana," the woman said. "A woman with such a fine-looking husband shouldn't have such heavy thoughts."

Braylin felt her lips twitch. Just the mention of Dugan made her smile, it seemed. Leana gave a little laugh.

"Oh, so it seems ye ken what a prize ye have there in yer husband," Leana continued. "Glad I am to know it; else I would have to take this moment to share my unsolicited opinion."

"You are bold," Braylin remarked.

Leana looked straight at her. "Is that a chastisement, Mistress?"

Braylin wrinkled her nose. "Please do not call me that."

Leana drew in a breath and let it out in a little sigh. "It seems I will be giving ye my opinion after all. Ye are failing to appreciate the way that husband of yers is trying to make certain ye know how much he adores ye."

"Adores me?" Braylin asked in a stunned whisper.

Leana nodded. "He surely does. Shavon is a fool not to see how he looks at ye. She'll not be head of house for long."

The weight that had been threatening to crush her all day suddenly lifted. "How can you be sure?" Braylin asked.

Leana fixed Braylin with a very pointed stare. She appeared to be debating how to answer.

"I know men," Leana stated bluntly. "And the ones who have no affection for their wives, or respect, well that is the very sort of man that I have a great deal of experience with."

Leana's expression was hard and in her eyes was bitter understanding.

"How did you come by so much…experience?" Braylin knew she sounded naïve, but the topic was so very important to her.

Leana locked gazes with her. Braylin could see the other girl debating whether or not to answer the question. But Braylin didn't shrink away, but stared straight at Leana.

"My father settled a rather large gambling debt with my maidenhead. After I was ruined, my sire discovered there was money to be made in installing me at a brothel where he and the whoremaster shared my earnings."

"How despicable!" Braylin exclaimed. "The commandment to honor one's parents was never intended to be used in such a way."

Leana stared at her for a long moment. There was a look of disbelief in the other woman's eyes which baffled Braylin.

"Who wouldn't be horrified by such a tale?" Braylin asked.

"Many are very horrified," Leana answered. "But they normally look at me as though I am some pestilence which must be driven away before I smear my grime on them. No one ever considers my feelings."

Braylin felt her cheeks heat. Her father and mother would have forbidden her to even look at Leana after knowing she was a woman for hire.

Well, didn't you want to have a different sort of life here?

Braylin lifted her chin, squared her shoulders and smiled at Leana. "Thank you for answering me."

"Ye are very interesting, mistress," Leana said. "Truly I am surprised by yer nature."

"Good," Braylin responded firmly.

A feeling was growing inside of her. Braylin wasn't sure just what it was, only that it felt amazing—almost as though she'd just discovered that she liked herself. Was it pride? Possibly. But she really wanted to think it was confidence.

Confidence was something she might use to build the life she wanted.

"Yer husband sees ye as his wife, not as English." Leana said, offering up her opinion as she'd promised. "His demand that ye sit and be served is his way of demonstrating to one and all that he will not have ye viewed any other way. Ye need to see the blessing there."

Braylin felt the truth of Leana's words sinking deeply into her. "Thank you," Braylin muttered.

Leana lifted one eyebrow in disbelief.

"Why would I not thank you?" Braylin asked, adding a sincere smile.

Leana looked straight at her. "Because I am a whore," she said frankly.

Braylin thought for a moment. "Didn't you arrive with me?"

Leana's expression became guarded. "I did."

Black Moss Tower had a large number of men compared to the number of women serving in the towers.

"Is someone here forcing you to continue to perform such a trade?" Braylin asked. "For if they are, I will have them put out immediately."

Surprise flashed in Leana's eyes. "Well, in order to do such a thing, ye would have to be the mistress of Black Moss Tower, now wouldn't ye?"

Braylin smiled and nodded firmly. "No one will be forced to do such a thing, as long as I am here."

Something flickered in Leana's eyes—hunger perhaps?

Braylin straightened her shoulders. "It is close to supper time. We should not be late."

⟫⟩⟨⟨

LEANA REMAINED IN the storage room for a time after Braylin left.

She felt odd, as if something was fluttering inside of her. A feeling that was so precious, so fragile, she feared to even breathe lest it be crushed.

Hope.

It seemed a lifetime ago that she had felt it. Back when she was a girl who had looked at the future as something bright and full of possibilities. Oh yes, she'd seen the challenges ahead of her.

But she had always believed there'd be a chance for her to find happiness.

It hadn't taken long for that hope to be snuffed out. Whores faced a lifetime of knowing their greatest worth was behind them.

Leana moved to the doorway of the storage room, watching as Braylin walked up to the main towers. The flicker of hope she suddenly felt seemed to be growing stronger, maybe even strong enough to burn away some of the bitterness which had built up inside of her.

Leana started across the yard to see if Braylin would take her place at the head table.

Today, she would hope for a brighter future.

And it appeared that Braylin was intent on making good on her word. She watched Braylin lower herself in front of Dugan— though she didn't miss the fact that Braylin had her hands tightened into fists that were hidden in the folds of her skirt.

Dugan and Braylin were the center of attention and neither one of them faltered.

Leana smiled brightly—a smile of respect. True, freely given, and well-earned respect for Braylin.

Her mistress.

EVERYONE WAS AT supper.

The main hall of Black Moss Tower was bursting at the seams. If there was even one retainer missing, Braylin would have been surprised.

And they were all watching her.

Let them.

Braylin felt as though her spine was stiffening, keeping her upright and proud. She fixed a pleasant expression on her face before she walked straight to the high table where Dugan was watching her from behind one of his unreadable expressions.

She didn't mind though. There was great satisfaction in knowing she was holding her own tonight. Braylin stopped in front of Dugan and lowered herself into a curtsey.

"Welcome, Wife," Dugan greeted her.

Braylin rose, walking around the table to take her seat. Ryesen was there along with Erin. Once Braylin sat down, the supper service began.

She had never sat during the first service of a meal.

In her father's house, she had carried a pitcher of water while Modesty had held a basin and Temperance had come last with a cloth. As the daughters of the house, they had helped their father and mother wash their hands before their eldest brother brought the bread to their sire for the blessing.

Everyone had a place in the service of the meal. Tonight, even those sitting at the head table had a place as well in the ceremony.

She would be the mistress of Black Moss Tower. Her duty was to serve everyone by ensuring order and fairness. If even one of the lowest scullery maids went without stockings, it was Braylin's failing. The mistress ensured everyone's needs were met while they served.

She would ensure there was enough in the storage rooms to feed them all until the next harvest. It was a heavy responsibility and one which required obedience from the staff to see it accomplished. For if there was no order, the inhabitants might gorge themselves upon the supplies and exhaust them before they might be able to replenish them.

Yes, a heavy burden but one she would not fail to carry.

Because Braylin was very certain she would rather die than see the hope in Leana's eyes crushed.

BRODY SNIFFED BEFORE pouring himself another serving of whiskey. The hall was quiet as men bedded down. In the kitchens, the four boys who helped out with the heavier chores were curled into the bunks they were afforded.

The female staff were all in the storerooms, so Brody sat quietly at the long table used for producing the meals during the day. Now there were long hollowed out sections of logs sitting on that table top that had the next day's bread dough rising in them.

Brody looked up to see Dugan entering the kitchen.

"Ye have a new wife," Brody remarked. "What are ye doing here, lad?"

Dugan sat down and reached for the bottle. "I'm thinking."

The sound of the whiskey filling a glass was the only thing heard for a moment. Brody watched as Dugan lifted the glass to his lips.

"She did well at supper," Brody continued.

"Aye," Dugan agreed.

"Just as ye bid her," Brody added.

Dugan took another sip of whiskey. This one was longer. When he lowered the glass, there was a tight set to his jaw. It was clear he was wrestling with some demon. Brody held his tongue, waiting for Dugan to speak.

It took another couple of sips of whiskey before Dugan admitted, "Me wife does nae want to run this house like Lady Alice."

Whatever Brody might have expected Dugan to say, that wasn't it. "I will drink to that, lad!"

Dugan didn't raise his glass. His fingers were turning white because of how hard he was gripping it. "I ordered her to the table, to be served as the mistress of Black Moss Tower. Just as Lady Alice does each night."

Brody contemplated Dugan for a time. "The pair of ye have to get to know each other and that is a fact."

Dugan reached for the bottle, but Brody plucked it from the tabletop. "This is not the answer, lad."

Dugan's eyes narrowed.

"Go on with ye now," Brody instructed. "Nothing will be worked out unless ye are in the same room together."

Frustration glittered in Dugan's eyes, but he grunted and gave Brody a nod. His friend grinned in victory.

"Do nae think ye are so very clever and fooling me," Dugan muttered with a grin. "Ye are drinking to avoid a woman as well. Perhaps ye should take yer own advice, Brody. Young Erin has certainly been trying her best to make it clear she wants to be courted by ye. Leave the lass fluttering her eyelashes at ye here and she'll be at the church doors before the end of the winter on the arm of another man."

BRODY STARED AT Dugan in surprise. Dugan sent his man a knowing look before he tightened his resolve and headed above stairs to where Braylin was.

Would she welcome him?

He hoped so.

The stairs were narrow and dark. Dugan made it up to the

top floor and opened the door.

He knew she was there.

It was strange the way he was so very aware of her. There was only the faintest sound of her breathing, but the chamber had her scent.

It stirred him.

And drew him toward her. She'd left one side of the bed curtains open for him. When he tugged the length of fabric free, she drew in a stiff breath.

"Oh…I fell asleep," Braylin muttered.

Dugan joined her in the bed, closing the curtain. "Rest lass. Morning will come soon enough."

Braylin rubbed her eyes. "I was waiting for you, Dugan."

"Ye do nae have to worry if I am pleased or not, lass." Dugan settled on his side facing her.

Braylin sat up. "You have been kind toward me. I would have you content with this marriage you were trapped into." Then she let out a little sigh, as if she'd faced something she knew she needed to and yet struggled to find the courage to do it.

"In truth, I need to thank my lady stepmother," Dugan confessed. "For she saved me from wrestling with the idea of returning to the borderland to make ye mine."

"My father would not have received you," Braylin said.

Dugan raised an eyebrow, his expression becoming mocking. He reached out to smooth a piece of hair which had fallen in front of her face. "But I would have returned to try and tempt ye to run away with me. I am yer Laird of Misrule, lass."

He heard her draw in a little breath. The sound sent a ripple of desire through him. "It's a fact that I enjoy making ye gasp, Braylin. There is a wildness inside ye that I hope ye do not curb completely, even if there are times I must ask ye to rein it in."

"There are advantages to being the mistress of the house," Braylin said, surprising him. "Wrongs that I might set right, yet only if I shoulder the duty of the position. Managing the household will take strict attention to details. I will do my best to not shame you."

Dugan cupped her jaw. "We shall shoulder the load together, lass."

He leaned in to kiss her. With the bed curtains closed, sinking into her embrace was the only thing Dugan was interested in. Later he'd remember to ask her what wrongs needed righting.

For now, he could succumb to his need for her.

CHAPTER NINETEEN

L EANA WAS IN the kitchen at first light.

Braylin smiled in welcome. The other staff was stirring slowly, for a storm had closed its grip around Black Moss Tower during the night. Outside, the wind was swirling. The clouds were so low, they seemed to touch the very ground. Tufts of snow, just starting to fall, would soon become a blanket of white on the ground that would stay until spring.

It was magical.

Bitter for sure, yet there was a freshness to the air which matched the happiness fluttering inside her.

"I'll gather the eggs."

Braylin didn't give anyone a chance to argue with her. Her belly was rumbling, and Leana was bent over near the copper, lighting the fire which would bring the water up to boil. A hard cooked egg sounded perfect to Braylin, so she lifted a basket off the table and went out the back door.

Her cheeks tingled.

And her breath came out in a puff of white.

The hens didn't think it was too cold. The birds were out, searching for bugs or worms to eat. They began to cluck, hopeful that she was bringing them some kitchen scraps to eat.

"You will not be disappointed," Braylin said. She emptied the basket onto the ground to the delight of the chickens. They lunged in toward the vegetable and apple skins, pecking at them.

Getting the eggs would be much easier now.

Braylin headed for the far side of the walled-in yard which was behind the kitchens. Here, there were nest holes built into the wall. A couple of hens who had still been inside their nests squawked in annoyance when they realized that they were missing a treat.

Braylin reached inside the boxes, searching for fresh eggs. She worked her way along the wall and out of the opening to where a few more nests were. Now that the season was changing, these nest holes would likely be abandoned but the hens, with their coat of feathers, were not yet cold enough to share the inner nest.

She found two eggs and stretched up onto her toes so that she might reach into the back of a hole that was on the high, arched portion of the wall.

Suddenly, a hard thud hit her on the back of her head. Braylin dropped the egg onto the ground. She felt the pain traveling through her like a bolt of lightning so bright, it was blinding. When it hit her between the eyes, she dropped like a stone.

LEANA USED A wooden plate to fan the growing fire beneath the copper.

The flames caught and grew brighter with the addition of more air. She watched for a good amount of time to make sure the wood had caught, then, with a nod of satisfaction, she closed the door in front of the fire and straightened up.

Her lower back popped.

She smiled, looking at the water in the copper. The water, essential to the running of a kitchen, would simmer all day.

The hens in the yard started making a ruckus, their squawks hard and sharp in warning to one another that a predator was nearby.

Their little bird brains couldn't differentiate between those who tended them and a fox or wolf.

Leana looked toward the door, but Braylin didn't appear.

So, what were the chickens raising an alarm over?

A tingle touched her on her nape. The air was icy and the day gray. There was no reason for Braylin to linger in the yard.

A jaded life had taught Leana to look closer at things that didn't seem right. Seeing the wrong thing easily translated into an untimely death for someone like herself.

But Braylin had looked at her without judgement. A need to be worthy of that stirred inside of Leana. Perhaps Braylin had slipped on the icy stones while trying to carry a full basket of eggs.

Leana moved to the door and looked out. The hens were all near the opening in the wall which went around the kitchen yard. The birds were still agitated, their feathers raised while they talked to each other about something Leana couldn't see.

Leana looked behind her, but the kitchen was empty. The boys had gone to the stables to help with the morning chores and the other women were being slow about rising. She stepped into the yard and walked toward the opening in the fence. The basket was there, on its side, with fresh eggs scattered all over the ground. Some had cracked, proving they'd fallen.

But Braylin was not there.

Leana looked around and caught sight of two men carrying Braylin off in the far distance, looking as if they were about to disappear into the woods. She had only a moment to decide to follow or risk their direction being lost because the snow was coming down so hard. There was no time to run back into the kitchen to raise the alarm and the snow wasn't thick enough to leave a trail.

Leana surged forward, hurrying to close the gap between her and the men who had her mistress. As the snow crunched beneath her feet, she unsheathed a small cutting knife that was on her belt and began to cut bits of her arisaid off to use as a trail. She sliced her finger because she was looking at the men, but Leana didn't stop.

Whoever they were, the mistress wouldn't last long in their keeping.

DUGAN EXPECTED HIS wife to be at the table.

But Braylin wasn't there. Shavon spotted him the moment he arrived though, proving that the head of house had taken his warning to heart. The sound of her snapping her fingers at the maids bounced around the inside of the hall.

Dugan caught sight of Erin. She was walking toward the head table, carrying a pitcher.

"Where is yer mistress, Erin?" Dugan asked.

Erin looked up at him. "I've just come from the stables with the milk, as is my assigned duty."

There was an edge to Erin's tone. She looked toward Shavon.

The head of house was quick to defend herself. "The mistress has not yet given any instructions on who shall be her personal staff. This is a small house with a large number of retainers to feed. There is a great deal to be done each day to see the table filled and the mud kept outside the doors."

Dugan felt the muscles between his shoulder blades tightening up, promising him pain from the tension. Truthfully, he had been too harsh in his thinking toward his father's plight.

Running a household was beyond difficult.

But something else was bothering him. Dugan dismissed his irritation with Shavon in favor of trying to identify what it was that was needling him. There was a burning in his gut that he'd learned to trust. He swept the hall once more. The tables were back in the middle of the space. The retainers were sitting down as the maids dashed back and forth with the first meal of the day.

Braylin was not among them.

The empty place beside him bothered him greatly. That sensation in his gut turned into a sense of foreboding.

Dugan stood. His chair skidded back, making a loud skidding noise. Conversation died down and his men turned in his direction to see what he wanted.

"Who has seen my wife this morning?" Dugan asked.

Most of the retainers had slept in the hall, so they hadn't yet gone outside. They looked at one another, but no one spoke.

"I saw her—the mistress…"

Dugan wasn't sure who had spoken. He looked around the hall, his attention settling on one of the kitchen boys. The lad was tall and rail-thin, proving he was not one of Shavon's personal friends. His shirt was patched and frayed and the sleeves were a full two inches too short for his arms. When He realized Dugan was looking at him, he snatched his bonnet off his head and nodded in respect.

"I saw the mistress going out to collect the eggs." The lad's voice was steady and strong now. He had obviously found some courage.

Dugan headed for the passageway which connected the hall with the kitchen. Brody was at his back. Shavon had spoken true, for the kitchen was full of women in a flurry. There was a crash when one of them dropped a bowl because she'd been startled to see the master of the hall heading into the kitchen looking so intent.

Dugan didn't have time to reassure her.

"Where are the hens?" Dugan demanded.

The woman who had dropped the bowl was halfway down to the floor to pick up the mess. Her eyes were large and wide in her face. She lifted one hand and pointed to the far side of the kitchen where there was a door.

Dugan pushed it open so hard the door hit the outer wall of the kitchen. Outside the snow was swirling. He strode straight forward without flinching.

Braylin was nowhere in sight.

There was a spot where scraps had been left for the hens. The snow hadn't covered it yet and a couple of birds were still pecking hopefully at it. Most of the birds had moved away, telling Dugan that too much time had passed since Braylin went to gather eggs.

"Dugan—the basket." Brody pointed toward the end of the yard which enclosed the kitchen. Just a corner of a basket was in sight through the opening.

Eggs were scattered on the ground, snow sticking to them. Dugan felt his belly heave. He looked up but already knew too much time had passed for him to catch sight of whoever had attacked his wife.

Worse yet, the snow was only now collecting on the ground, so there were no tracks. He wanted to rage against the unfairness of it but didn't dare waste the time to do it.

He knew life wasn't fair. The best a man might hope for was to have the cunning to keep his wits about him when he had something to face.

He turned and looked at Brody. "Get someone up to the mews to see if the master saw anything or if there is sign of a trail."

Most of the retainers had followed them outside. Brody pointed at one who tugged on his cap and turned so fast his kilt swirled away from his body before he charged off to complete his task.

Most of the maids had followed as well. One of them was already rushing to gather up the eggs. Dugan caught sight of Erin.

"Erin, come here," he said, pointing at the girl. She gasped but Dugan didn't have time to be compassionate. The retainers thrust the girl forward, closing their ranks behind her.

"Who else came with ye to Black Moss Tower at me step-mother's direction?" Dugan demanded.

Erin was terrified.

Dugan hardened his heart against the girl's terror. He stepped toward her. "Tell me who took my wife."

Erin was shaking her head. Fear seemed to have made it impossible for her to get a word out but his men weren't letting her escape. They formed a solid wall behind her, lending their hard looks to Dugan's demands.

"Speak up girl." Brody squeezed her shoulder.

Erin let out a squeak. "Letters....I was just told to write letters! I would never hurt the mistress! Never!"

The maid was shaking. Dugan swallowed the bitterness trying to soften him toward her. When it came to Braylin, he would do whatever was necessary.

"Who else arrived with us?" Brody looked at the surrounding group. "All of ye... Out here where I can see ye."

It didn't take very long. The retainers who had been at Black Moss Tower knew one another well. They parted and pushed the newly arrived members of the household forward. Dugan swept them all, looking for any sign of nervousness.

"Where's the lightskirt?"

It was Shavon who asked the question. Men parted so that Dugan could see the head of house. Shavon looked straight back at Dugan, clearly eager to earn some goodwill from him.

"There was a lightskirt here," Shavon informed him bluntly. "She likely didn't think I knew what she was, but a head of house needs to know details. I made certain to check into everyone who arrived with ye."

"And yet ye failed to tell me Lady Alice had sent her personal maid." Dugan cut Shavon's attempt to gain glory for herself off at the knees.

Shavon wrung her apron for a moment but gathered up her composure rather quickly.

"The lightskirt...Leana..." Shavon pointed at the people standing in front of the retainers. "She is not here, and she was newly arrived along with ye. There isn't any reason to look further. A woman who sells those types of services is not one to be trusted."

The wall of retainers behind Shavon was not pleased. Their expressions were dark and in their eyes was a promise of retribution.

"Make way. I have word from the master of the mews..."

The retainer Dugan had sent was trying to break through the wall his comrades had formed. He ducked down low and managed to make it through, looking very much like a fox who had discovered a hole in a fence. When he popped up, his eyes glittered with achievement. He swallowed and became serious.

"The master of the mews said he saw a woman heading off into the woods…" The young man pointed behind Dugan. "Half an hour past. He thought it strange, with the snow starting to fall, but said she was hurrying toward the woods as though someone was chasing her. Or she was chasing someone else."

Dugan turned and went to where a maid was standing with the basket of eggs. He reached in and took one. He held it in his hand judging the warmth. Brody joined him, along with a couple of other experienced retainers. They each took an egg to make their judgements on much time had passed since Braylin had dropped the basket.

"We'll not be able to use horses in the woods," Brody said.

"So close to the kitchen, a cry would have been heard," another retainer stated. "They likely knocked her out."

Dugan fought the urge to growl. He needed to be level-headed. "Carrying her will slow them down."

"Aye," Brody agreed. "But in the woods, there will no' be a trail to follow."

Dugan knew it. The forest was thick. It would take a long time for enough snow to accumulate and form a blanket on the ground.

Whoever had his wife had planned the attack well. He didn't want to waste time thinking but a battle took brawn and wits to win.

And this was going to be the greatest test he'd ever faced.

"WE DO NAE have time to rest, Ewan."

"I'm the one hauling dead weight, Murdo."

When she was dropped onto the ground, Braylin regained consciousness, but the pain in her head was blinding.

"We're far enough out," Ewan continued to argue. "Killing that bastard will be simple here. After all, we have his woman to draw him in close."

Braylin gasped. Remaining quiet would have been smarter, but the thought of Dugan being killed tore her heart in half. That pain was a thousand times more than she could bear silently. Her own safety didn't matter if Dugan was in danger.

There was a snort above her. She opened her eyes to get her first look at the two men who had abducted her. They stood over her, sneering at her like they might an unwanted dog.

"Get up," Murdo ordered.

Ewan seemed motivated by the idea of not having to carry her. He reached down to grab a handful of the arisaid Braylin had wrapped around her head and shoulders. Her knees were still a little weak when she made it to her feet, but she squared her shoulders and refused to show any weakness.

She could not allow Dugan to be drawn in.

"Dugan will consider himself well rid of me," Braylin informed them. "You are wasting your time if you believe he is going to venture out in the snow to follow me. He'll likely think I ran off. I've done it before."

Murdo contemplated her from behind an expression that was quite terrifying. Braylin found herself comparing this man and Oran. For as frightened as she'd been when taken from her family, Braylin realized that Oran had never looked at her with hatred in his eyes.

Murdo and Ewan both regarded her as something which had no worth. She was a burden to them.

"He wed ye when his father said he did not have to," Murdo said. "He'll come for ye and when he does, we'll put a final end to the threat against our lady's bloodline."

Bloodline. That was something men *did* kill over. Lady Alice was a Sinclair, and her blood was fine enough to see her sitting side by side with the Laird of the Hay.

Braylin felt her heart thumping hard inside of her chest. She'd managed to become the perfect bait to lure Dugan to his death.

But how to dissuade them?

"Lady Alice will have you killed...to cover her own plot," Braylin said, finally managing to get her brain to work. But her voice was too tight, betraying how desperate she was.

Murdo raised an eyebrow. "Look closer, woman. We are Sinclair. Our laird will be very pleased to know the pestilence his sister has suffered from is at long last dead. But just in case yer husband is not passionate enough to be clumsy in his approach...."

Murdo reached out and grabbed a handful of Braylin's skirts, yanking her forward. She stumbled, unable to keep her footing. There was a flash of a blade. Murdo pulled a small knife from the top of his boot and sliced her neatly across the top of her lower arm. The blade of the knife was sharp, separating the wool of her sleeve to expose her skin so he could spill her blood.

Braylin recoiled, twisting and turning, trying to wrench her arm from his grasp. Her efforts were in vain. Worse than that, when she looked at Murdo's face, she saw the cruel little twist on his lips which told her how much he was enjoying her plight. The glitter in his eyes made her belly heave.

He turned her wrist over so that her blood dripped onto the snow.

"That should serve to make yer husband just worried enough to make our job simple." Murdo smiled brightly. He looked up at the ridge in front of them. "Let's climb some more. Dugan Hay is strong in a fight. We need to make sure we take him from the high ground."

Braylin tried to resist, but Murdo was too strong. He reached out and bound her wrists together with a length of rope, then started off, pulling her along. The rope was rough and when she resisted, it dug into her flesh until the pain was too much to bear.

She stumbled after him, forced into obedience.

Don't come for me… Don't come….

Even as she prayed, Braylin knew Dugan wouldn't heed her. Even if it was only duty which fueled him, she knew he would not fail to come after her.

And she would be the bait which lured him to his death.

CHAPTER TWENTY

DUGAN PAUSED AFTER only a few steps into the forest.
He didn't want to stop, but there was no way to know
what direction to take. Brody and the others were peering
intently at the branches, looking for signs that men had passed
through.

Dugan was grateful to have their help.

And he was proud too, for these men knew the highlands and
the wilds. Tracking was an art, and they were accomplished in it.

It was still going to take divine intervention for them to find
Braylin.

Dugan closed his eyes, seeking help from heaven. It was by
far the most sincere and earnest prayer he'd ever sent.

When he opened his eyes though, the thicket was still a mass
of branches and limbs that appeared to all run together. He
backed up to the edge of it, thinking to look at the bigger picture.
The forest remained unchanged but something next to his foot
grabbed his attention.

Dugan bent down. What had first appeared to be just another
dead leaf sitting on top of the snow was, in fact, a little curl of
cloth. It had landed on a little patch of new snow, making it stand
out. The scrap was thin but when he opened it, Dugan saw the
distinct colors of the Hay tartan.

"What is it?" Brody asked.

His friend ventured close, squatting down so he could see
what Dugan held. Something was needling Dugan, a feeling that

he was close to what he sought. All he had to do was see the path to take.

He looked back toward the kitchen yard. Five paces away, there was another little curl of fabric sitting on the new snow. Brody got up and headed toward it. He picked it up, flattening it to see that it was indeed another little slice of Hay tartan.

"It's a trail," Dugan announced.

The rest of the men gathered around to look at the two scraps.

"It might be bait," one of the retainers cautioned.

"Aye, but it is the direction I am heading." Dugan faced his men. "Braylin is me wife. I stood at the church doors of me own free will. I will not order any man among ye to join me, for I have not yet earned yer loyalty." He turned toward the forest.

"Yer lady has proven herself a worthy mistress in noticing the injustices being done by the head of house. I will help to bring her home."

Dugan turned his head to see every retainer ready to follow him. Just which one had spoken, he wasn't sure, but they were all nodding in agreement. The determination on their faces was more praise than Dugan could ever recall being directed toward him.

He hoped to be worthy.

But it would be worthless without his wife. She was the other half of his soul.

"I found another scrap," Brody called from inside the forest. He held it up.

Dugan went toward it as if it was the very light of heaven shining through the darkness. Even if it was a trap, it was the way to Braylin.

And nothing could stop him from going to her.

"THIS IS THE spot," Murdo announced.

Braylin ordered herself to maintain her composure, but it felt like she was trying to swallow an apple, whole. Still, she had to keep her wits about her.

She had to find a way to warn Dugan.

Murdo was looking up the trail and back down it. He appeared to be judging something.

"Watch her," Murdo ordered Ewan. He handed the end of the rope to him.

Ewan nodded, winding the rope around his hand to prove that he had a firm hold on it. He waved his partner onward while he caught his breath, his breath coming out in little puffs of white. Murdo climbed up the side of the ravine, disappearing from sight, but Braylin heard the crunching of the snow beneath his footfalls.

They were heading nearly straight up. The steep incline had been cut by the flow of water that ended in a river somewhere down below them. Far, far below them.

Ewan was still panting. Braylin looked at the incline.

Could she just pull him off-balance?

You might break your neck on the way down.

It was a risk she was willing to take. Braylin reached out and caught the rope between her fingers, then widened her stance, getting ready to yank on the rope with every bit of strength she had.

There was a snap behind her, heralding someone's approach.

Ewan reached out and grabbed her skirt, yanking her in front of him. "Ye stop right there, or I'll slice her throat!"

Someone was coming up the trail. Braylin could see them through the thick limbs of the trees that still had needles on them. "They are going to kill you, Dugan!" she cried out, not caring about her own safety.

"Quiet!" Ewan barked, dragging her backwards. His knife was at her throat, the blade stinging her when it cut into the delicate skin.

She smelled blood and dug her fingers into Ewan's arm.

"There is another, Dugan… Another man. They were sent to kill you!"

Ewan was panicking, pulling her in different directions. Braylin caught a glimpse of a figure on the trail. Braylin heard a soft whoosh and then a cry of pain.

Ewan snickered. "Ye hit the mark Murdo!"

Braylin was suddenly free. Ewan shoved her to the side with a little whoop of victory. He scrambled down the trail, his knife raised up high to finish the job.

No…

Braylin lunged after him. She collided with his back, knocking Ewan off his feet. Then they both started tumbling down the steep trail.

DUGAN HEARD A woman cry out.

The sound pierced his heart. It sounded like a fatal wound. He hung his head. He would not—could not—accept that Braylin was dead.

Not yet.

He scrambled up the trail toward the sound. Ahead of him, he saw a woman crumpled on the ground, twisting and turning while clutching at an arrow that had pierced her shoulder.

There was yet hope to be had.

"Braylin!" Dugan shouted. The last few steps were longer than miles. He dropped down beside her, seeing nothing but the bright red blood covering her.

"She's there…up there…." Leana gasped out a warning.

Dugan pulled his attention off her wound to look at her face. "Leana?"

Before he got the chance to think about what Leana was doing there, another whoosh split the air. Leana hooked her fingers into his coat, pulling him down on top of her.

"Archer!" Dugan cried out the warning to the men behind

him.

Dugan knew he had precious little time before the archer might fit another arrow into his bow. He pushed up off Leana and rolled over his shoulder, stopping in a crouch. The archer would be looking for any movement before he loosed his next shot. Dugan tried to catch sight of the man, but what he saw were two bodies tumbling down the trail. They landed near Leana, the man snarling as he fought to get his feet beneath him.

"Ye bitch! I am going to enjoy slitting yer throat!" Ewan declared.

The man was about to carry out his threat. Dugan saw the naked steel of his blade when he raised his arm.

Before he could drive the blade home, Dugan sunk his fist into the man's exposed belly. Ewan's breath escaped in one hard sound. He sagged over Dugan's shoulder as two more arrows cut through the air. He felt Ewan jerk when the arrows sank into his back.

But Ewan wasn't about to die. He bared his teeth and brought his knife down toward Dugans's neck.

Time had a strange way of slowing down when men were spilling each other's blood. Dugan had experienced it before. Today was the first time he was glad to be ending a life, because this man had touched his wife. Even if he had to die himself.

It was a cruel fate, for he'd only just learned to live for himself.

But the blow didn't land. Dugan felt his lungs inflate with another breath and looked to the side. A pair of bound wrists were at his eye level. Braylin met his gaze as she held Ewan's arm up in the air as he finally succumbed to the arrows, and his life seeped out of him.

Without a doubt, heaven had answered his prayer.

EWAN SLUMPED TO the ground, lifeless and Braylin didn't feel any remorse.

She stared at Dugan, fearful of moving, least she pop the bubble they were encased inside of. Here, he was alive. But there was movement around them. She blinked, noticing the other retainers and Brody.

Several men had charged up the trail after Murdo.

"Here lass, let me cut this binding," Dugan muttered softly.

He handled her bound wrists carefully, expertly inserting his knife blade into the space between them so he could cut the cords of rope binding her.

"Good riddance," one of the men muttered as he gave Ewan's body a soft kick.

"How did you find me?" Braylin asked.

"Leana followed you," Dugan answered.

Braylin looked around, remembering the cry she'd heard. Leana was sitting on the ground, while Brody used a strip of cloth to bind her shoulder. The arrow was on the ground, its tip bloody and the shaft broken in half.

"Ye're doing fine, lass… Just bear with it," Brody encouraged Leana.

Brody had always seemed such a hardened warrior. She'd never had guessed the man had a softer side.

But she was witnessing it now as he knelt at Leana's side, kindness etched into his expression.

Braylin suddenly realized how many retainers were there. "Thank you." Her voice was just a croak. Heat burned her cheeks as embarrassment nearly strangled her. "I was not careless, I promise you. Truly, I am sorry to have put you all in danger."

"You owe no apology, lass." Dugan touched the side of her face to gently turn her toward him. "No man was ordered to come with me."

Braylin felt her eyes widen. She turned her head back to look at the assembled retainers. They all reached toward their caps to tug on the corner in respect.

"Ye have earned the respect of yer house, Braylin, something Lady Alice has never done."

Braylin looked back at Dugan. "Murdo and—" Her gaze went toward Ewan. "—and Ewan. They were Sinclair. They wanted to kill you, to prevent your bloodline from threatening Lady Alice's children. I was simply bait."

Dugan grunted. "They made a mistake in bringing their fight to Black Moss Tower." He curled his fingers around her forearms to keep her close to him. "I'd kill anyone who tried to harm ye. Ye are more precious to me than the breath in me lungs, Braylin."

"Precious?" Braylin asked in a whisper. "I was forced upon you, and now, you nearly died because of me."

Dugan slowly shook his head. "Ye have shown me how to love, Braylin. It is a deeper love than I have ever known in me life!"

"You...love me?" Braylin realized she was shaking. "How...it isn't possible. I was thrust upon you. Your family honor was at stake."

There was a snort from Leana. "Laird Hay sent me here to destroy your faith in your new husband by compromising him. There was no honor involved."

Braylin looked over at Leana in shock. Now that she was tended, the woman had gotten to her feet and stood staring back at Braylin.

"Oh, Leana, I have failed to thank you," Braylin exclaimed.

Leana lifted an eyebrow. "You are the first person who has treated me with kindness and respect. I will happily suffer ten more wounds if it means ye are safely recovered. Black Moss Tower needs ye as its mistress."

"Aye."

"Well said."

"Ye are a fine mistress."

The compliments turned her head for sure. But Braylin discovered that what stirred inside of her wasn't pride, but gratitude, and with it came the desire to always be worthy of the looks she saw on the retainers' faces.

It would a lifelong task and she fully intended to be devoted to it.

BRAYLIN WAS IN her own bed.

With her husband.

She smiled. She was exhausted and yet, she didn't want to surrender to sleep just yet. No, she needed to savor the moment.

"Why are ye not sleeping, Wife?" Dugan asked from beside her.

Braylin turned and saw Dugan, on his side, his head resting in his hand, watching her.

"I am still marveling at the fact that I am here with you," Braylin answered honestly.

His lips twitched up at the corners. As far as smiles went, it was small but there was so much genuine feeling in the little expression, she felt breathless.

But there was a hard look in his eyes.

"Forgive me," Braylin muttered. "This is a grave matter concerning your family. I do not mean to make light of it. You must be torn over how to proceed."

A little hint of surprise entered his eyes, but his smile grew larger. "Ye are worthy of the respect the retainers showed ye today, Braylin. Ye have a true skill for seeing and hearing the unspoken needs around ye."

She did? Braylin worried her lower lip while attempting to understand just what he meant.

Dugan chuckled. "Do nae worry wife. Ye are doing very well just being yerself. Yer mother would be proud of ye."

Her mother…

Braylin stiffened.

"Och…now I am the one forgetting facts." Dugan smoothed her cheek with his fingers. "Ye must miss yer family, lass. I promise to find a way to get a letter to them, but it will have to wait until spring."

Braylin realized Dugan was watching her intensely.

"Many brides travel away from their homes," Braylin said, trying to be cheerful.

"But not by force." Dugan's eyes glittered with renewed anger. "Lady Alice has gone too far this time. I cannot allow her wicked schemes to be swept aside again."

"Are you taking Murdo to your father?" Braylin asked.

Dugan's face tightened. "Ye deserve justice, Braylin. I understand ye must think I should hang them—"

"I have everything I desire," Braylin said, interrupting him. "Right here in this tower—in this bed—I have far more than I ever dreamed was possible. My heart is too full to be troubled by anything."

"He should be executed." Dugan wasn't giving up so easy.

"That is not for us to decide," Braylin said, adamant.

Dugan's eyes narrowed. "He took ye from me, Braylin." His gaze lowered to the thin cut on her neck. "And I am in charge of ensuring this house is secure."

"He only followed the orders of his laird," Braylin answered. "So…take him to your father and let men of station deal with one another. I will be most content to live here at Black Moss Tower, well away from all of the power struggles."

"As would I, lass, but as master of this place, I have to protect those who live beneath its roof." Dugan nearly growled with his frustration. "Lady Alice will not stop until I am removed from the line of secession."

Braylin knew he spoke the truth. She thought for a moment. "Do you not have a brother?" Braylin asked.

"Aye, but in Scotland, a grown son might always take the lairdship if there is an untimely death. My father became laird in just such a way," Dugan explained. "I suppose there is a valid reason in the way Lady Alice is forever concerned over the matter. She could not rightly cry foul if her place was taken away in the very same fashion as she landed there. More than one would say it was justice."

"And you would live your life always looking over your shoulder," Braylin said.

"Aye, and I want none of it," Dugan declared.

Braylin wanted to believe him. She searched his eyes, seeking confirmation.

"What is it ye want to see, lass?" Dugan asked her softly. "I have already told ye that a life here with ye is all I crave."

"But you barely know me at all." Braylin failed to keep her emotions from spilling out. "Perhaps you should just keep Murdo here for the winter and think upon the matter...."

"I love ye, Braylin." Dugan laid his hand alongside her face to make certain their gazes were locked. In his eyes, she saw that truth. "Murdo must be dealt with—that is my duty as the master of this house. No one should ever believe that attacking a member of this house will go unpunished."

"You are correct. Duty must be done," Braylin agreed. "For this house will be better for both of us facing the more unpleasant aspects of running it."

Dugan surprised her by grinning. "Does that mean ye are agreeable to remaining my wife?"

Braylin felt her cheeks heat. "I confess, I am well and truly under the spell of the Midnight Well. My heart is yours in this life and the next."

"Eternity..." Dugan whispered against her lips. "Only eternity is long enough to suit me."

BLACK MOSS TOWER had cells within its bowels.

Hours after Braylin had fallen asleep, Dugan found himself unable to join her in slumber. He wasn't sure what he was doing, only that his restlessness had refused to be sated and now, he was on his way to where Murdo was being held.

Was he about to spill the blood of the man who had dared to take his wife?

Dugan didn't honestly know. But he wanted to think he was more than a blind follower of rage. The hot flash of vengeance never lasted very long. And when it was burnt out, a man had to find a way to build a future in the very same world where he'd allowed his temper to ignite.

As much as he loathed them and their actions, he knew it would be wise to keep the Sinclairs at his side. Just how to accomplish that was what was needling him so badly that he couldn't sleep.

Lady Alice had failed to have him killed. So now, Dugan was going to make his own path.

He wandered down the narrow steps, winding his way beneath the hall to where the cells had been built. They had been dug out of the solid stone the towers were built upon, and had been intended to hold those who crossed the border between clans.

The moment Dugan made it to the ground floor, he heard the grating sound of chain on the stone.

"Come to see me in the dead of night?" Murdo asked.

There was more grating. Murdo materialized from the darkness of one of the cells. A thick chain attached to a shackle around his foot. The light from the torch Dugan held flickered and danced, illuminating them both.

Murdo looked past Dugan.

"So ye've come alone, bastard?" Murdo chuckled softly. "Ye must want something from me. I won't betray the Sinclair."

Dugan placed the torch into a holder on the wall. In spite of the arrogance on Murdo's face, the man looked at the torch with a little gratitude in his eyes. He jerked his attention away from the dancing flames when he realized Dugan was watching him.

"Speak yer mind, bastard," Murdo grumbled. "Not that it will do ye any good."

Dugan was silent for another moment. "What crime was Laird Sinclair willing to pardon ye from for doing this chore for him? There couldn't have been many volunteers. Sinclair retainers might spill blood on the battlefield when needed, but this is far different—more of a coward's way, taking a man's wife and spilling his blood when he comes for her. I'd be surprised if some of your fellow Sinclair retainers would welcome ye back after committing such a foul deed. Who would want to close his eyes next to you, knowing what ye will do to further yer own cause?"

Murdo spit on the ground in answer. "I had the better end of the bargain. I promise ye that, bastard."

Dugan looked around the dungeon. "From the look of yer circumstances, I don't find myself agreeing with ye."

Murdo snorted. "Are ye here? Without yer men and a priest?" he chuckled. "Ye are…because ye don't dare kill me. Fine, ye have me chained but at some point, ye will have to give me back to yer sire and he will not cross the Sinclair. Every house has spies. Me kin will learn of me fate, have no doubt about that."

Murdo crossed his arms and leaned against the rough rock wall. "One winter is a fine trade for what I needed in return."

Murdo's attitude made Dugan's temper flare. The desire to spill the man's blood was almost too great to resist.

But a leader always used his head.

"Since I do nae want anything from my sire, I don't need to court his good favor," Dugan answered.

"Every man needs his family," Murdo answered seriously. There was a hint of bitterness in his tone. "We all do what we have to in order to please those set above us. Ye'll bend too. But ye already know it. That's why ye came to see me alone. Displease yer laird and ye'll lose Black Moss Tower."

It was the truth.

Dugan battled the rise of his frustration. He needed to think, to find another way. He and Braylin had come so far—he had to find the path which would lead them to the future he'd promised her.

Murdo was still smirking but there was bitterness etched into his face as well. "Ye are no stranger to obeying Lady Alice," Murdo muttered. "Her brother is no' any easier to serve."

Whatever Dugan had expected to find in the dungeon, a compatriot wasn't it. But Dugan didn't care for how much he had in common with Murdo.

Which meant he had to change the way he dealt with Lady Alice. It would be a very dangerous move on his part, but Dugan realized that boldness had served him very well since the night of the bonfire.

So perhaps that was the path that he was looking for. It might also lead him to ruin. But he'd rather die with his chin held high than live the way Murdo was willing to.

Honor was a gift a man gave himself.

Hay Castle

CORMAC LOOKED UP to see Dugan entering the great hall.

"Dugan lad!" Cormac greeted him from the high table. "Come and warm yerself! What are ye doing riding in this weather?"

Dugan didn't smile at his father.

None of the men with him smiled either.

Cormac noted the lack of warmth and his smile faded.

He heard the clink of chains, then watched as Brody stron-garmed a shackled man forward.

"The Sinclair—" Dugan said, speaking loud enough for everyone in the Great Hall to hear him. "—sent two of their own to kill me at Black Moss Tower. The other one is dead."

Cormac tightened his fingers into fists. "By Christ, they will pay! Black Moss Tower is Hay land!"

Around them, the Hay retainers grumbled, their discontent

clear. Cormac gestured to Dugan. "Come to me study. The rest of ye, eat yer fill."

Dugan followed his father into the study. Once the doors were closed, his father eyed him suspiciously. "What game are ye playing, Dugan?"

"No game, father." Dugan stared straight back at his sire. "Ye charged me with running Black Moss Tower. The Sinclair found it a perfect opening to rid Lady Alice's children of any threat to their inheritance."

Cormac was silent for a long time, obviously weighing all possible outcomes before speaking. He was a true laird.

"I do not want to be laird of the Hay," Dugan stated clearly. "It is time to have that put on parchment for all to see."

"You crave that English wife of yers over being laird?" Cormac asked pointedly.

"I do," Dugan answered immediately. "I will swear fealty to Rohan before the clan."

Cormac grunted.

"Father…" Dugan softened his tone. "My English wife brought to my attention how much fear there is in this house. Isn't it time to be done with it? Must ye be as close to yer death as Laird Lindsey before ye realize life is meant to be lived now?"

Cormac pointed at Dugan. "That English wife has brought forth the man in ye, Dugan."

Dugan smiled. "She has. And she craves peace. If I swear fealty to Rohan, the Hay will be settled. Everyone will benefit from that peace. I am content with what ye have given me. In the spring, we'll begin building a fine house. There is naught more I crave."

Cormac flattened his hands on the top of his work table. "Aye, it's a fine thing to see ye content with Black Moss Tower. Ye will be its Chief. Rohan will be fortunate to have ye standing guard on the flank of his land."

"DUGAN WILL DO what?" Lady Alice sat back, her jaw hanging open.

"Ye heard me," Cormac said, giving his wife a hard look. "We'll have the ceremony tonight. Dugan wishes only to return to Black Moss Tower before the snow gets any deeper."

Lady Alice started to smile.

"Do nae preen, Alice," Cormac warned her. "All ye have done is to blacken yer name, and that of the Sinclairs. All of yer scheming will be a weight on Rohan's shoulders because he has yer blood in his veins."

"I was protecting his position," Lady Alice argued.

"Ye are a fool." Cormac leaned closer to her. "Dugan has found a way to earn the clan's respect while on his knee. Rohan has naught earned that loyalty. Men do nae follow leaders who have not earned their trust. Yer brother has wagered and lost. I will never name ye Regent, for it would be signing me own death warrant."

His wife went pale. She sat back without further argument, at last accepting defeat. But her hand settled on her belly, a soft motion which drew his gaze.

"Aye," Alice muttered sounding defeated. "Yer babe is growing in me belly once more."

Cormac snorted. "Perhaps that is what is needed—something for ye to concern yerself with. Be done with yer schemes, Alice, else I will have to have ye under guard."

"Ye will not!" Alice growled at him.

Cormac stared straight back at her, unwavering in the face of her temper. "So long as ye carry that babe and let Dugan be, I will not sequester ye. But this is yer final warning. I am the laird of the Hay."

Cormac went back to the closed doors of the chamber, pounding on one with his fist. A retainer outside opened it.

"Lady Alice may attend the swearing of fealty if she so chooses," Cormac told his men before he disappeared down the steps.

Alice sat for a long time, torn between the need to refuse to witness Dugan gaining any approval from the Hay retainers and the desire to watch her son stand up straight as the next laird of the Hay.

Her mother's heart won the argument.

Alice stood and hurried out to watch her son take his rightful place.

CHAPTER TWENTY-ONE

Black Moss Tower

LEANA GROANED. SHE had tried to stretch out her hand to pick up a comb, but pain tore through her, leaving her collapsed against a pillow.

"Ye moved," Brody chastised her.

Leana blinked and rubbed her eyes. "What are ye doing here?"

Brody set a bowl and a plate down beside the bed Leana was resting in. "Making sure Shavon understands that ye are me personal friend."

Leana narrowed her eyes. "The mistress says I have a place in the household. I will not be earning my keep on me back."

Brody sent her a hard look. "I did not ask to hire ye, Leana."

Leana let out a little frustrated sound. "I know what a man means when he calls me his friend. Go on with ye. I've seen the way young Erin looks at ye. Be done with women like myself. Court that girl and wed her."

Brody slowly smiled.

The curving of his lips cut Leana deeply. Honestly, she'd thought her heart was dead, but the way Brody's eyes glittered with appreciation gutted her.

"I thought ye just told me that ye are no longer that sort of woman. Daft wench. It's you I plan to take to the church doors." Brody reached over and picked up the bowl, then used a spoon to gently stir the contents. Steam rose up, filling the air with the scent of stew.

"Me—?" Leana opened her mouth and Brody popped the spoon into it.

The stew was delicious. In spite of doing nothing but resting all day, she was ravenous. Spitting the food out was out of the question. She chewed and settled for sending Brody an aggrieved look.

"Erin is a sweet girl," Brody said, stirring the stew again. "But I am not a sweet man." His voice had a hard note in it. Leana recognized that tone, for it came from having experienced the same harsh realities that she'd had.

She opened her mouth, but Brody had the spoon at her lips again. No one had ever fed her. Well, perhaps someone had when she was an infant, but she couldn't ever recall it happening since. Brody, with his scarred forearms and hard features, was the most unlikely candidate for bedside service.

Yet he was there.

Feeding her stew.

Whatever that meant, Leana decided she wasn't about to squander the moment on thinking.

DUGAN SAT DOWN on the step outside his chamber door. A sensation rippled through him—one he was unfamiliar with. What was it? A sense of homecoming? That was indeed a first for him. Suddenly the ache in his lower back was worth suffering, for it had helped him create the place that was far more than just a sturdy roof to cover his head.

Home.

Hearth and family would follow if he was lucky. Many might think it wrong that his misadventures as the Laird of Misrule would offer up such a good ending, but understanding came to him as he sat upon the step. Nothing came from nothing. The life he had with Braylin was the result of him straightening his back and going out to build a better future.

A man lived on his knees or found the courage to stand and face the onslaught of the world. He would have had nothing more than a life of begging at Lady Alice's hem unless he tried to find something better.

And so, he had.

That was true for women too, he decided. Braylin had risen to her position through courage and determination. He was blessed beyond his wildest dreams to have such a partner beside him in life.

It would be warm inside the chamber, but it was near midnight, and he didn't want to wake Braylin. He worked to untie his boots. His fingers were stiff with cold, so he had to rub his hands together several times to accomplish the task.

He eased the door open, creeping into the room, and closed it carefully. Dugan smiled, feeling victorious but when he turned around, he found Braylin looking back at him through the open curtains on the bed.

His smile grew. Dugan reached up, touching the single feather on his cap that was pointed upwards. It was just a small one, but the significance was large.

"Welcome home, Chief," Braylin said, marking his new rank.

The bed ropes creaked when he climbed into the bed alongside her.

"So ye have heard?" Dugan asked.

"A bird was sent to tell us the news," Braylin confirmed. "Are you happy?"

Dugan gathered her close, tipping her chin up so their gazes met.

"I've become my own man, Braylin. We will have a good life here. In the spring, I will begin building ye a fine house."

"I have all I need," Braylin assured him. "We do not need to spend the money on a house."

"Me father insisted," Dugan informed her. "The silver comes from Lady Alice's own coffers. A gift given on the day that I pledged my loyalty to her son."

"That is...um..." Braylin obviously didn't know what to make of that.

Dugan tucked her head beneath his chin. "It is as perfect a solution as we might have ever gained. We'll have a fine house and with God's blessing, a fine large family to fill it."

Dugan heard her mutter a soft agreement against him.

All was well.

His wife was by his side.

Nothing else mattered.

Nothing at all.

Spring – Black Moss Tower

ERIN MADE A pretty bride.

With her hair brushed out and the May sunshine shimmering off its glossy length, she began her walk toward the church. After a long winter, the inhabitants of Black Moss Tower were eager for entertainment and merriment. Men tucked new spring heather sprigs into their bonnets while the women wore crowns of woven greens.

By the time Erin and her groom made it to the gates, there was a long procession behind them. Everyone was happy, their feet light. Three pipers led the group, playing an old tune on their reed instruments while a young lad helped keep time with a drum.

Leana was nervous.

Even with Brody by her side, she discovered herself looking around, waiting for someone to sneer at her.

No one did.

Instead, they all witnessed the vows of the young couple.

Here in the highlands, customs were slow to change, so Erin and her groom stood at the doors of the church for the blessing. Even the priest smiled while he performed the rite.

There were whoops and cheers when it was all over. The music began again and everyone joined hands to begin dancing in a huge ring. Shavon presided over a hogshead of mead, making certain each person received an equal measure of the brew.

"Leana, there you are," Braylin called out.

Leana started to lower herself. Braylin waved her hand.

"How many times must I tell you to stop with that?" Braylin asked.

Leana tilted her head and smiled. "As many times as we must remind ye to sit and rest, Mistress."

Braylin rubbed a hand over her rounded belly. "I feel brimming full of energy."

"Well, ye are full of something, for sure."

They all turned to see a man wearing a different tartan walking up beside Dugan. Off in the distance, his men followed.

"I see the winter wasn't nearly as cold here as it was on Lindsey land," Ruben Lindsey said, sending Dugan a smirk.

Dugan grinned without a hint of shame. "A wife makes for a fine, warm winter indeed my friend. I suggest ye try it." He put his arm around Braylin. "Ruben is on his way to the border. He can deliver letters to yer family."

Braylin gasped. "Truly?"

She didn't wait for an answer but twirled around and headed off toward the towers. Leana and several others rushed after her, all intent on ensuring Braylin didn't tumble due to her advanced pregnancy.

Leana managed to get around in front of her before Braylin made it to the steps leading up to the tower where her bedchamber was. Leana pointed at her.

"I will fetch the letters, mistress," Leana stated.

"There is naught wrong with me," Braylin insisted.

Just then, her baby decided to give a hard kick. Braylin rubbed her distended belly, distracted by the motion. She'd always thought she might become a mother someday, but the reality was so much more vibrant than her daydreams.

There was only one thing lacking in her life. When Leana returned with the bundle of letters, Braylin felt tears stinging her eyes.

Telling her family that she was safe was the last thing to be done. The carefully folded letters were addressed and tied with twine. She turned around, intent on hurrying back to where Dugan and Ruben were but they'd followed her up to the towers.

"I'd be grateful if you would see these to my family," Braylin said.

Ruben reached up and tugged on the corner of his bonnet before he took them from her hand. "It will be done." He tucked them into his doublet before he went to the tables to join his men in enjoying the meal that was laid out in preparation for the returning wedding party.

"Here now, lass," Dugan said, wiping the tears off her cheeks with gentle motions. "I thought to make ye happy."

"You have." Braylin smiled up at him. "You have made me happier than I ever believed possible."

Their gazes locked and once more, Braylin felt as if the entire world simply disappeared. There was only her and her Laird of Misrule. Both of them had been enchanted the night they'd met by the Midnight Well. And they planned to remain that way for the rest of their days.

The Border

RUBEN WAITED FOR moonrise, enjoying an early season apple he found growing along the way. Because he'd been so close to the border, he hadn't tempted fate by stopping to hunt and cook something to fill his empty belly. The fruit was a gift which he received with a nod of thanks sent upwards toward his guardian angel.

Ruben finished off the apple before he emerged from the forest surrounding the Midnight Well. He slid off the back of his horse and gave the animal a pat on its neck. The horse made a low sound before walking closer to the well.

"Thirsty?" Ruben asked jovially. "I am as well."

He pushed the cover which sat on top of the well halfway across its opening. The scent of fresh water rose up to tease him and his horse. The animal pawed at the ground and snorted some more.

"I'm hurrying," Ruben assured his mount.

He dropped the bucket down, heard it splash when it hit the surface of the water, and then he began pulling on the rope. Getting the water back to the surface was the part which required some strength.

Ruben pulled hard, smiling when the bucket came into view. He leaned over to grab it by the side, hoisting it up by one side. The bucket tipped, allowing some of the water to trickle out over the rim. Ruben saw the water droplets beading up as they fell back into the dark well but there was something else. On the surface of the water, he saw a reflection.

Ruben narrowed his eyes, trying to identify what he was seeing on the surface of the water. The fluid stopped moving while his hand was frozen on the rim of the bucket. The surface of the water went as smooth as a polished glass mirror affording him a reflection of a girl's face.

She was perfect.

There was no single feature which stood out, for she was simply dressed. But Ruben felt as though a beam of light had broken through the veil of night to illuminate the reflection just so that he would always see her face.

Something snapped. Ruben dropped the bucket, breaking free of the strange enchantment which had made him stare at the contents of the bucket instead of realizing there was someone on the other side of the well. He jumped back, landing in a fighting pose.

The girl gasped, shuffling back a few paces. Her eyes were wide, making him instantly feel guilty for frightening her.

"Forgive me, lass," Ruben said, making an effort to soothe her. He'd never been so sincere or worried that his apology wouldn't be trusted.

"I did not see you, sir," she muttered. "Until I was too close."

And he hadn't heard her. Ruben would chastise himself later for failing to hear the lass approaching. For the moment, though, he was captivated.

And tongue-tied.

His horse snorted once again. The girl looked at the animal and smiled.

"Your horse is thirsty," she said, pushing the cover of the well back toward Ruben. She reached for the rope that was tied around a beam above the opening of the well, then began to pull the bucket up.

"Let me do that, lass." Ruben reached for the rope but only managed to grasp her fingers because she didn't release it.

A current of awareness jumped between them.

A sensation that felt too strong to be real.

And yet, Ruben knew she was just a girl, not some mythical creature roaming the forest beneath the moonlight. Nor had he drunk too much cider. Whatever passed between them, she seemed to feel it as well, quickly withdrawing her fingers and clasping them against her chest while she blinked.

"Who are ye, lass?" he asked.

"I am Modesty Hawlyn."

Her name sunk in, helping Ruben to resume thinking. "Yer sister sent me here."

"My sister?" Modesty questioned.

Ruben nodded. The bucket was once more at the top of the well. He lifted it up and placed it on the ground so that his horse might at last have the drink the animal craved.

"Aye." Ruben reached into his jerkin. "Braylin has sent ye a letter. I promised to bring it to ye."

"Braylin," Modesty whispered the name almost reverently.

She hurried around the well, not stopping until she was only a single pace from him. Ruben found himself fascinated by her, to the point that he failed to release the letter when she attempted to tug it from his fingers. A little furrow appeared in the center of her forehead.

"Apologies, lass," Ruben said, regaining his senses. She succeeded in pulling the folded and sealed parchment free, then smiled.

Her smile was more pleasing than anything he'd ever seen.

"Modesty?"

Someone was calling from down the hill.

"You must go." Modesty forgot the letter and looked at him. "My brothers will raise the alarm and you are a Scot."

Whoever was looking for her called again. Ruben reached up and tugged on the corner of his cap.

"My name is Ruben Lindsey, lass."

"Well…yes. But you are a Scot. So hurry on your way please. I do not care to see you dragged into the market square for stopping to water your horse."

Ruben was tempted to stay right where he was. But in her eyes, he saw true concern. If he stayed, he'd be risking more than his own suffering and for once, that mattered to him.

"Until the next time we meet, lass."

"Oh we can never meet again," Modesty scolded him softly. "Please stay well away from here. There is a new garrison of soldiers here to secure the border." She extended her arm, pointing behind him. "Go, sir, and be careful. This is not a safe place."

"Braylin says yer father is devoted to his Puritan faith," Ruben said.

"He is."

"Any garrison sent by the queen would also be intent on

enforcing the return to the Catholic Church."

Fear drew her features tight. "My father says we must remain faithful to the Puritan path."

Ruben extended his hand out. "Come with me, lass."

He was mad to make such an offer, and yet, there was no stopping the words. Even knowing how insane he sounded, Ruben didn't regret his invitation.

She started to reach for his hand—Ruben knew he didn't imagine it. But her name came from down the hill again and she turned and started running toward whoever was searching for her.

Ruben had never been so close to tossing a lass over his shoulder in his life.

There was a soft chuckle from behind him.

Ruben turned to see an old woman standing there, watching. She smiled widely, showing off her gap-toothed smile.

"You saw her in the water," the woman declared as she pointed at the moon that was now rising above the treetops. "In the light of the full moon. If you eat the fruit of the forest and look into the water of the Enchanted Well, you will see the face of your soulmate."

It was nonsense, of course.

So why did Ruben look back down the path Modesty had gone, feeling as though he'd just lost a part of himself?

About the Author

Mary Wine has written over twenty novels that take her readers from the pages of history to the far reaches of space. Recent winner of a 2008 EPPIE Award for erotic western romance, her book LET ME LOVE YOU was quoted "Not to be missed..." by Lora Leigh, New York Times best-selling author.

When she's not abusing a laptop, she spends time with her sewing machines...all of them! Making historical garments is her second passion. From corsets and knickers to court dresses of Elizabeth I, the most expensive clothes she owns are hundreds of years out of date. She's also an active student of martial arts, having earned the rank of second degree black belt.